*A word from Sydney Stone,
ex-plain-Jane:*

I won't even go into the reason why I was
staying alone at the hotel to begin with—
way too sordid! I'll just say it had something
to do with my gorgeous, glamorous sister and
some compromising photographs. The next
thing I know, I get that little note from "T,"
and suddenly I'm in the Starlight Lounge,
then I'm mysteriously transformed from a
plain-Jane into a glamour-puss and running
around doing things with the sexiest man I've
ever seen. The kinds of things Sydney Stone
from the suburbs would never do in real life.
Except now this *is* my real life....

*Dear Reader,*

Imagine: you're at home when a carrier pigeon delivers a note to your window. A love letter, perhaps? No—a "Dear John" letter…meant for the gorgeous groom-to-be next door. And *you* have to deliver the bad news.

That's how Jillian Horton ends up saying "I do" to Cord Dougald in bestselling author Cait London's *Every Groom's Guide To….* The happy newlyweds are just settling into married life when the modern bride learns that her lovable groom is the most old-fashioned man she's ever met. Surely he'll accept a few lessons in "Modern Husband 101," right?

Now imagine this: you're staying in a hotel when you mistakenly receive a seductive little note and a key in an envelope: *"Sweetheart—meet me at the Starlight Lounge at 10—Love, T."* In Kathy Marks's *Seducing Sydney,* plain-Jane Sydney Stone can't resist meeting the mysterious "T," if only to tell him his note was delivered to the wrong woman. And that's how Sydney is seduced on the adventure of a lifetime….

Next month, you'll find two Yours Truly titles by favorite authors Marie Ferrarella and Jo Ann Algermissen—two new novels about unexpectedly meeting, dating…and marrying Mr. Right.

Yours truly,

*Melissa Senate*
Editor

Please address questions and book requests to:
Silhouette Reader Service
U.S.: 3010 Walden Ave., P.O. Box 1325, Buffalo, NY 14269
Canadian: P.O. Box 609, Fort Erie, Ont. L2A 5X3

# KATHY MARKS

## Seducing Sydney

Published by Silhouette Books
**America's Publisher of Contemporary Romance**

**SILHOUETTE BOOKS**

ISBN 0-373-52018-2

SEDUCING SYDNEY

## About the author

**KATHY MARKS** believes that odd and unexpected twists of fate do happen and that they do, in fact, influence people's lives. And what could be more unexpected than a letter from a stranger? As her character Sydney Stone discovers in *Seducing Sydney*, love can be a game of chance and every decision a roll of the dice that can change a person's life forever.

Kathy, still a newlywed, lives in Arizona with her husband, John, and her two dogs—Murdock the shelty collie and Dugan the Scottish terrier— who insisted they be included.

**To Sharon, who always understands
and who always laughs at my jokes,
even the clunkers**

## 1

You have deeply ventured;
But all must do so who would greatly win.

—Lord Byron

Sydney Stone leaned against the far end of the hotel desk, away from the festive commotion and brilliant dazzle of the casino floor behind her, and read her messages in surprise. Oddly enough, it wasn't the note from the blackmailer that held her attention. She'd been expecting that. His directions to wait in her hotel room for his call after midnight— she supposed most blackmailers kept late hours—was the message she'd been waiting for. Nor was she particularly concerned about the three frantic telephone calls from her sister, Sheila, who had always lived in a perpetual state of emergency and who considered anything connected with her own well-being a matter of extreme urgency.

It was the third, unexpected message—the envelope containing a small gold-plated key and a few hastily scrawled lines on hotel stationery in an obviously male hand—that made her wrinkle her nose and mutter to herself in puzzlement. As soon as she read the short letter, she pointed out to the desk clerk that the envelope, though bearing her room number—203—was obviously not for her. However, the young man behind the desk merely shrugged disinterestedly and picked up the ringing phone beside him, leaving

Sydney holding a misplaced love letter that she had no idea what to do with.

She read the words once more:

> Sweetheart. Where are you? Something went wrong.
> Meet me at the Starlight at 10:00 p.m. I *have* to see you.
> Love,
> T.

By no stretch of the imagination could she pretend the note was intended for her, Sydney admitted. The only person who ever called her sweetheart was her great-aunt Ruth from Modesto, and she'd been dead a good five years or more. Furthermore, other than the blackmailer, whom she hadn't yet met, she didn't know a single soul in Las Vegas, with or without the first initial "T."

It was a quandary, but not a completely unwelcome one. At least this new puzzle contained elements of intrigue and romance. Not like the business she came to look after which was definitely sordid, although not without its humorous side.

Pondering what to do with the mysterious love letter, Sydney hesitated by the front desk, turning the small key over in her fingers.

Making a sudden decision, Sydney pushed away from the desk and made her way across the casino floor toward the hotel elevators. The casino floor was as noisy as a carnival, with the ringing of electric bells, the jingle and rattle of coins and the constant din of voices and laughter. Everywhere, lights glittered and flashed, twinkling from chandeliers high overhead and beckoning from the sea of slot machines beyond the gambling tables. Purposefully, Sydney squeezed past the excited throngs standing shoulder-to-shoulder around the crap tables, wove through the crowds jostled together in the aisles between the rows of shiny slot machines and skirted the breathless group staring with hopeful gazes at the spinning Wheel of Fortune.

In her faded summer dress, which had once fit tightly and now bagged around her, and her brown-framed glasses and mousy blond hair pulled back by a rubber band, she blended easily with the tourists who had come to try their chance with Lady Luck. No one gave her a second glance as she waited by the elevators to be whisked up to her hotel room.

Actually, she would have been surprised if anyone *had* noticed her. After all, it was common knowledge among her friends and family that Sydney, although a terrific pal, was a singularly unremarkable woman. It was a fact she had long ago come to accept and now treated with a certain amount of good-natured amusement.

As she waited for an elevator, Sydney toyed again with the tiny key, wondering what it might unlock and if the man who sent it would tell her. Because, of course, she meant to go and give it back to him. The thought of some poor, lovelorn fellow waiting in vain all night for his lover to show up was too much for her secretly romantic soul. No, she'd decided to keep the appointment at the Starlight and return the letter to its sender. And why not? She'd be back in plenty of time to receive the blackmailer's phone call.

She entered an elevator and punched the button for the second floor. Going to the Starlight tonight, she thought contentedly, would be her good deed for the day. If nothing else, good deeds were her specialty, the only thing she'd ever really been proficient at.

Besides, what else was she going to do to occupy her time? Gamble? As the elevator doors closed, she smiled at the idea, imagining the looks she'd get if she laid down her measly savings—quarters and crumpled single-dollar bills, hoarded from several weeks' worth of tips. No, as alluring as it might seem from the sidelines, she wasn't a gambler.

There was only one thing that Sydney didn't consider. In Las Vegas, everyone was a gambler. Even for a down-at-the-heels waitress from Venice Beach, every choice could be a game of chance. Even the smallest decision was a roll of the dice that could change a person's life forever.

By the time Sydney stumbled through the doors of the Casbah, the casino where a helpful doorman had assured her she'd find the Starlight Bar, she was flushed, breathless and perspiring from her long stroll down Las Vegas Boulevard. Although the sun had set hours ago, the Strip was as bright as it had been that afternoon. Neon lights lit up the boulevard and the day's heat, rising in shimmering waves off the street, seemed to have been trapped by the miles of pavement. The very air seemed baked.

Just inside the gleaming glass doors of the casino, Sydney paused, dazed by the sudden blissful coolness. If her sister ever had another run-in with a blackmailer, she thought wryly, wiping a damp strand of hair from her cheek, she hoped he lived someplace cooler. Like Greenland.

Fixing the strap of her oversize purse more comfortably on her shoulder, Sydney wandered around the tables under the huge vaulted ceiling and got lost in the endless acres of slot machines. Finally, she stopped an employee to ask for directions. The man's name tag identified him as a "host," but he was unlike any host Sydney had ever seen. He was certainly nothing like tiny red-haired Ellen who was the hostess back at Little Vernon's Bar and Grill where Sydney had waited tables for the past five years. In a dark pinstriped suit, the man gazed down at her, his height and enormous bulk blocking out even the light from the chandeliers above them.

"The Starlight?" he asked doubtfully, repeating her question.

"Yeah, you know. It's a *bar*." She gazed levelly back at him. "I'm meeting someone there."

"You are, are you?" The man looked her over critically, skepticism evident on his large, broad face as he took in her wrinkled dress and disheveled hair. "You sure you want the Starlight?"

"Of course I'm sure," she said impatiently. "I just said so, didn't I?"

With a shake of his head, the big man relented. "All right, lady. Go through the casino, up those stairs and down the hall to the elevators. It's on the fifteenth floor. Once you get off, you can't miss it."

As Sydney moved away, he called after her with a disconcerting snigger of laughter, "Good luck, lady."

If she was mystified by his laughter, she understood the moment she stepped off the elevators. With its elegant marble pillars, the entrance to the Starlight was imposing. Lofty black-glass doors, no doubt tinted to discourage the average tourist from accidentally wandering in, guarded the inner sanctum, impressive and intimidating. As she stood hesitantly in the center of the hall, the doors to the bar opened and a couple passed through. Sydney caught a glimpse of a dimly lit, low-ceilinged room. A faint wisp of perfumed air and the soft, muted strains of a jazz tune wafted out. Then the doors swung shut.

Feeling awkward and conspicuous, Sydney watched the lean, suntanned man and the young woman in a startlingly short black dress get onto the elevator she'd just exited. As the doors closed on them, the man put his tuxedoed arm around the woman's slender waist and threw back his head to laugh. Despite Sydney's smile at the couple, neither had given her a glance.

*Oh boy,* Sydney thought nervously. She was definitely out of her depth here. Self-consciously, she looked down at her faded dress, covered with large tropical birds, that had seemed so gay and colorful to her just that morning. Then she noticed her toes. Sticking out of her sandals, they were dusty from her long walk. Surreptitiously looking over her shoulder, she rubbed each foot against the back of her legs.

For a brief, panicked moment, she almost gave up the whole idea and headed back to the elevators. Then she thought of the man waiting inside the Starlight, and her curiosity gave her strength. *Just inside those doors,* she told herself as she straightened up and smoothed her hair. *Just past those doors is a world you've never seen before. If you chicken out now, you might never have another chance.*

She was going to feel like an idiot. She already knew she was going to look horribly out of place, but her curiosity to glimpse how the "other half" lived was stronger than her fear of humiliation. Steeling herself, she reached for the door handle and pulled.

Stepping through, Sydney came to a halt, blinking blindly at the sudden darkness of the bar. With a start, she caught her own reflection from across the room. At first, she thought her glasses must be smudged because her image was so hazy. Then her eyes adjusted to the lighting, and she realized she wasn't facing a mirrored wall but a stunningly wide stretch of windows. Below, the lights of Las Vegas twinkled and winked like a thousand sparkling jewels scattered carelessly across the night.

Dazzled by the beauty of the scene before her, Sydney sighed with pleasure and smiled. Sitting at low, carefully arranged tables, couples in evening dress, men in dark, expensive suits, and women in glittering sequins talked and drank. There was something hushed and muted about the place despite the murmur of voices, the clink of ice on glass and the seductive fluidity of the music, as though the bar itself was awed by the sheer luxury and wealth it exuded.

Trying to pretend a self-assuredness she didn't feel, Sydney headed across the lush carpeting toward the bar as though she'd visited the place a hundred times. With as much aplomb as possible, she hung her enormous purse over the edge of a low-backed bar stool. When the weight of her purse nearly toppled it over, she perched herself on the edge with her purse in her lap, her face warm with embarrassment.

The bartender was about her age, twenty-five or so, but he fumbled inexpertly behind the bar, glancing anxiously at a small book as he carefully measured ingredients into a blender. Sydney pegged him as a novice. She hadn't worked in a restaurant all these years without being able to spot a rookie behind the bar. Her heart went out to him.

"Can I get you something?" he asked politely, laying a square white cocktail napkin in front of her.

"No, I'm not staying. I'm just looking for someone. A guy I'm supposed to, well, sort of meet."

He watched her wordlessly.

"Do you know if any of those guys out there," she asked, jerking a thumb behind her to indicate the tables, "are waiting for someone?"

"Are you sure this is the right place?" he asked, but without the sneer of the host downstairs.

"Yeah. It says here," she explained, pulling the envelope from her purse, "to meet him at the Starlight at 10:00 p.m."

"Well . . ." The bartender studied her uncertainly, then gave her a smile. "I'm new, so I don't know many of the customers yet. That man over there." He pointed. "He's been waiting for a blonde for about fifteen minutes. Said to send her on over."

Sydney sighed with relief. "Hey, thanks. Thanks a lot. And good luck with the new job." She almost added that she hoped no one ever stiffed him, then realized that *his* clientele probably always tipped big. "Which guy did you say?"

Turning, she looked in the direction he indicated.

"There. In the corner near the windows. Dark hair. Tuxedo."

"Oh." The word came out like a groan. "Him?"

The man sat alone, his long legs stretched out casually. He was in his early thirties or thereabouts, and very good-looking. In fact, Sydney thought, gazing at him from her stool, he was one of the handsomest men she'd ever laid eyes on. His thick, black hair was swept back from a high, intelligent forehead, and against the white of his immaculate dress shirt, his face was strong and darkly tanned. There was an elegant ease about the way he lounged in the low chair, an aloof self-confidence in his quiet survey of the room. The careless angle he held his glass, dangling from his fingertips over the arm of the chair, communicated an air of suave sophistication.

"Must be," the bartender said. "He's the only guy waiting for someone. Only guy alone, in fact. Somebody told me his name, but I was so busy, I forgot it. I do know he's a high roller."

About to jump off her stool, Sydney turned back. "A high roller?"

"Yes. Like most of the guests in here. You know, the big men. The ones who the casino wants us to treat with kid gloves. They fly in on their own jets, blow half a million at the baccarat tables without blinking an eye and fly out again. It's pretty amazing."

Sydney stared at the dark-haired man sitting alone by the windows. "Oh, Lord," she muttered.

"That your man?" the bartender asked as she pulled her purse onto her shoulder and prepared to make the long journey across the vast carpeted expanse toward his table.

"I'm afraid so."

By the time she got to the table, Sydney felt as if her legs were made of stone. Awkwardly, she stood beside an empty chair, determined to get her good deed over with as quickly as possible.

"Excuse me, mister. The bartender said you were waiting for someone?" She made it a question.

Slowly, the man turned his head and looked at her. His eyes were very dark, almost black, and the quickness with which they took her in belied his languid attitude. He raised one eyebrow quizzically.

"Yes," he intoned, stretching out the word expectantly.

"Thank goodness." She sighed. "I'm so glad I found you. I wasn't sure I would."

The quick glint of shrewdness in his eyes, mixed with a flash of amusement, made her trip over her words. *Good heavens,* she thought suddenly. *What was she doing here?*

When she sat abruptly in the empty chair, his eyebrows rose a fraction higher.

"Actually," the man said in a voice deep and cultivated, as rich as warm molasses, "the someone I've been waiting for is a *particular* someone. Not that it isn't nice of you to join me. Still, although it's been a long night, I'm fairly certain you aren't that person."

"Oh, yeah. I know that. That's why I came to find you," Sydney explained. "I got your letter by mistake."

The man closed his eyes briefly. "My letter?"

"Yeah. You sent it to the wrong room."

"I did what?" He raised his glass to his lips.

"That's why I wanted to find you. To let you know you made a mistake."

A small, barely noticeable frown creased the man's forehead, and he studied her skeptically. "I don't think I'm following you. Are you sure you've got the right person?"

"You're waiting for someone, aren't you? A woman? The bartender said you were the only guy in here waiting for a woman."

The brief glint of amusement she'd seen in his dark eyes was a steady glimmer of silent laughter now.

"The only one, hmm? I guess that must be just another example of my brilliant good luck this evening." His low voice was thick with humor as though amused by some private joke. "But I assure you, the woman I'm waiting for isn't you."

"I know that." Reaching into her purse, Sydney brought out the envelope and laid it before him. "Like I said, you sent this to the wrong room. Sorry. I just didn't want you to think she wasn't going to show up."

She watched as the man picked up the edge of the envelope with long, strong fingers, then she began to rise.

"The Sunburst, hmm?" Glancing briefly at hotel logo on the envelope, he tossed it back onto the table. "I didn't send this."

Sydney sat back down. "You didn't?"

He shook his head. "Afraid not. Wasn't me."

"Are you sure?"

"Absolutely positive."

"But—" Uncertainly, Sydney broke off. She gazed at the envelope, then across the wide bar filled with tables. If not this guy, then who?

The man studied her quietly. Reaching into the pocket of his jacket, he pulled out a slender, gold cigarette case, flicked it open with a thumb and offered it to her.

Perplexed, Sydney shook her head and looked across the room again. Maybe one of those two men sitting near the bar sent the note, she thought.

"Let me get this straight," she heard him say. Turning back to the man across the table from her, she wrinkled her nose as he lit a cigarette. "You traveled all the way over here from the Sunburst? To find the person who sent this letter and to give it back to him?"

Silently, she nodded.

"Why?" he asked.

"Why?" Sydney echoed.

"Yes, why. Why would you do that?"

"Because he'll be waiting. He might think she stood him up or something. Maybe he'll even be upset."

Suddenly, he smiled a wide, charming smile that made Sydney realize again how very handsome this man was.

"A romantic," he said as though this notion delighted him. "Quite a novelty. You're probably the only one in Las Vegas."

Sydney shrugged. "Yeah, well. Look, I'm sorry I bothered you. I really thought you were—"

With a wave of his hand, he stopped her from leaving. "Hold on a minute. You can't go from table to table asking every one of these men if he wrote your letter. Not in here. Not with this crowd."

There was, Sydney thought, some truth to his words. "I guess I'll just have to forget it then. It's too bad. I really hoped I'd find the guy."

"Here," he said, extending a hand. "Let me see it again. I didn't write it, but since you're here and my appointment isn't, why don't you join me for a drink?"

Sydney's eyes widened in astonishment. She wondered if he was making fun of her, then decided she didn't care if he was or not. Numbly, she nodded.

"Good." He raised his hand, and before she could take a breath, a scantily clad waitress was beside them.

"Yes, Mr. Ames? Can I get you anything?"

"My friend would like—" He paused and looked at her questioningly.

"Tomato juice," Sydney murmured. "On the rocks."

She saw a dark eyebrow raise again and bit her lip.

"Of course. And may I get you another, sir?"

"Please." Stubbing out his cigarette, he spread the letter out on the table between them, but instead of reading it, he gazed closely at her again. "Perhaps I should introduce myself. Jack Ames. I'm staying at the Sunburst, myself. In fact, considering the amount I just lost at the casino over there, you could say I'm almost a part owner."

Sydney's small smile was polite. "Gambling can get you into a lot of trouble. Oprah Winfrey had a show on it a while ago."

"Oprah Winfrey? Well, anyway, it's certainly true enough. Gave me about a hundred and fifty thousand dollars' worth of trouble tonight alone, I'd estimate." Once again, he gave her that disarming smile. "But then, it's all for a good cause, you could say," he added cryptically.

Sydney blinked at him, not certain she'd heard correctly. A hundred and fifty thousand? Is that what he'd said? In one night of gambling?

Amazed, she gaped at him, and for the first time since she'd entered the Starlight, a tiny thrill of excitement shivered through her. Just think, she told herself, she was sitting here in this luxurious place with a—what was the word?—a high roller. A high roller who was so handsome, he'd give any woman palpitations. Boy, would she have something to tell the other waitresses when she got home. They wouldn't believe she'd had the guts.

"And you are...?" he prompted as she accepted her drink from the waitress.

"Me? Oh, sorry. I'm Syd."

"Sid?" He looked disbelieving. "You're joking. That sounds like a bookie's name. What's wrong with your parents?"

"Well, actually it's Sydney. Sydney Stone. But everyone just calls me Syd."

"Not me. How do you do, Sydney Stone?" he asked gravely. "And where are you from, Sydney?"

"Venice Beach."

"Ah. Sunny California. Are you a surfer?"

A smile crossed Sydney's face at the thought, and she shook her head. "I'm a waitress. I *was* going to be a photographer. Actually, I'm still working at it. But until I make that first million or so, I figured why starve to death? So I wait tables at Little Vernon's Bar and Grill."

"I see. And you're here to try your luck at the tables, spend a few days at the pool and chase down confused men who can't send a letter properly?"

Uneasily, Sydney twisted in her chair. Nothing, she thought, could be further from the truth. This was no vacation for her—or at least, it wasn't supposed to be. Her sister would be appalled if she could see Sydney now. Sheila would have a royal fit.

"Yeah," Sydney agreed noncommittally. "Something like that."

"And how has your luck been tonight?"

"My luck?"

"Yes. Have you been winning?"

"Winning? Oh, *winning*. Well, I haven't done too much gambling yet. It's not really my thing, you know." She paused, not sure why she was telling him so much about herself, then added, "The only prize I've ever won was a toaster oven. When the new bank across the street opened up. And that shorted out a week later."

He smiled that devastating smile again, and Sydney began to relax. There was something reassuring and strong in Jack Ames's manner that made one trust him instinctively. He was easy to talk to, she decided, because he listened so well, as though he was actually interested.

"Sounds like my luck tonight. Still, anyone can gamble," he said. "The trick is knowing the odds and not fooling yourself into thinking you can beat them when you can't." He took a sip of his drink. It looked like scotch. "I could probably let you in on a few tricks of the trade. How much do you have to play with?"

"How much what?"

"Money. How much money did you bring?"

"Ten thousand," Sydney said without thinking. For a moment, she couldn't believe her own ears. Appalled, she gasped and raised a hand to her mouth.

"Then blackjack's your game," he said, seemingly unaware of her reaction. "Ten thousand's really not enough to risk on roulette or baccarat. You need to stay in for the long haul with those."

"Actually, it's not really *all* my money," Sydney murmured, wishing she'd never opened her big mouth. She wasn't about to tell him that *none* of it was hers. "And I don't think I feel too lucky right now."

"I could double it for you," he said with a confident smile.

"What?" Sydney blinked at him, then shook her head. "I don't think so, Mr. Ames. Didn't you say you just lost a hundred and fifty thousand dollars? Thanks, anyway, but you aren't exactly on a roll tonight, are you?"

"You have a point," he said amicably. "And call me Jack, please."

"Okay. Jack." Sydney sipped her tomato juice and looked around. "This place is pretty swanky, isn't it?"

He smiled. "Yes, I guess you could say that."

"Kind of gaudy though."

"It's Vegas. It's supposed to be gaudy."

Sydney nodded in agreement. "I sort of like it. It's sure a change from Vernon's, anyhow. I guess you must get used to it."

"Me?"

"The bartender said you were a high roller. You must come here a lot."

"A high . . ." Raising his face, Jack let out a deep, delighted rumble.

In a flash, Sydney was reminded of the man she had seen getting on the elevator outside the Starlight. The only difference was that she wasn't a beautiful, black-haired woman, and Jack Ames would never put his arm around her the way that man had put his arm around his date. Sydney sighed.

"How long have you been in Las Vegas?" Jack asked, still chuckling.

"Just today."

"Hmm. Yes, I thought so."

"Pretty obvious, huh?"

"Pretty much."

He was still smiling at her, and Sydney's heart missed a beat. Distracted, she fiddled with the envelope that lay between them.

"What are you going to do about that?" he asked.

"I don't know. I guess I'll give it back to the desk clerk. If he'll take it."

"Do you want my advice?"

"Sure."

"Toss it. Get rid of it. Forget you ever saw it."

Sydney dropped the letter as though it had burned her fingers. "What?"

"Maybe I'm an old, cynical high roller whose been disillusioned from living around the tables too long, but my interpretation of that note is a little different than yours. My suggestion is that you leave it alone."

"But why?"

"Let's just say it has a certain smell about it. At least to my nose. And I believe my nose is a little more experienced than yours."

Before she could reply, Sydney saw his eyes dart to the bar. Glancing in the same direction, she saw a slender, blond woman pause beside a bar stool, then slide gracefully onto the seat. Even without the floor-length, skintight evening gown that glistened with sequins, she would have been stunning.

Sydney finished her drink with one hurried gulp.

"Is she the one you've been waiting for?" she asked, nodding towards the woman.

"What?" he said distractedly, then looked back at her. "Would you like another drink?"

The way he'd stared at the woman at the bar had made Sydney feel a little ill. *How ridiculous can you get?* she chastised herself, trying to squash the feeling that seemed too suspiciously like jealousy. She was letting the atmosphere go to her head. For just a moment, she'd almost forgotten that the wealthy, beautiful world she was in wasn't hers.

This was just a fluke, a brief adventure, she reminded herself. And she had better quickly remember who she was *and* what she'd come to this city to do.

Pushing back her chair and taking the envelope from the table, Sydney rose. "Well, thanks for the drink," she said stiffly. "I better get going now."

He didn't try to stop her. "It's been interesting conversation, Sydney. I've enjoyed meeting you."

"Yeah. Same here."

Hesitating briefly, he reached into a pocket and took out a small white card. Laying it on the table, he scrawled something on the back with a thin, gold pen. "Listen, if you want some expert advice on gambling while you're in Vegas, give me a call."

Unhappily, Sydney took the card. His gesture, she realized, was one of politeness. He didn't expect her to call on him.

"Sure. Thanks a lot," she said, slipping the card into her purse.

All the way to the door, she had to fight to keep herself from turning and staring at the woman at the bar. A dull, aching hollow seemed to have opened in the middle of her chest, and her shoulders drooped miserably as she yanked on the tall, black doors.

Well, she told herself, that's what she got for getting above herself. But for just a few minutes back there, sitting across from handsome Jack Ames and letting him order drinks for her, she'd felt luxurious and pampered and…and almost pretty. What a fool she was to have let herself give in to the fantasy, even for a second.

It just made reality seem all the harder to take.

As the door began to shut behind her, Sydney couldn't resist one last, brief glimpse of that other world. Through the rapidly narrowing opening, she saw the gorgeous blonde from the bar throw her arms around Jack's neck with possessive familiarity and watched as he lowered his head to return her kiss.

Then with a thud, the door slammed shut.

# 2

―――◆―――

"And who," Belinda French asked as she settled in the chair opposite Jack, "was that?"

Jack leaned back in his own chair and considered the woman before him with real warmth. It had been so long since he'd seen Belinda, he'd almost forgotten how much he missed her... and Frenchie.

"*That*," he replied lightly, "was a mistake. She thought I was someone else."

"Uh-huh," Belinda teased, jangling the bracelets on her wrist as she reached for his cigarette case on the table between them. "Not exactly your usual type, is she?"

Jack flicked his gold lighter and lit her cigarette. "My usual type? I didn't know I had one."

"Oh, yes, you do. Everyone knows that."

"They do? And what, if you don't mind my asking, is my usual type?"

"Experienced." Slowly, Belinda blew smoke toward the ceiling. "And gorgeous."

Jack laughed with real pleasure. "Actually, she was an interesting young woman. There was something appealing about her. Fresh. Maybe I'm getting tired of 'experienced.'"

"And what about gorgeous?"

Jack thought about the woman who'd sat across from him only a few minutes ago, so nondescript in her saucer-size glasses and shapeless dress that he would have sworn her plainness was intentional. Yet for just a brief moment during their conversation, he'd thought he'd glimpsed something... well, something almost radiant in her. Like a shimmering mirage, a fleeting vision of loveliness that had nothing to do with physical beauty, the illusion had blinded him, stopping his breath, and then had vanished just as quickly, too quickly for him to say for sure what it was he had seen.

"Maybe 'gorgeous' has been a little overrated, as well," he said lightly. He caught Belinda's speculative look and grinned. "It *is* good to see you, Belinda. It's been a long time. Too long. I'm sorry about that. I should have called sooner or made some effort to... But somehow I felt that, with everything that happened—"

Reaching forward, Belinda laid cool fingers on his wrist. "It's all right, Jack. I understand. After Frenchie died, I didn't want to see any of his old friends, either. Not the ones who might remind me too much of him. Who might remind me that he wasn't here any longer. I expect you've felt the same. You loved him as much as I did."

Jack stared at his whiskey glass, turning it around in his fingers and remembering with painful vividness the last time he'd seen Belinda's husband—the time that had made her a widow.

"Yes. I did." He took a long, fortifying drink and once more changed the subject. "So, tell me, how are the twins?"

Belinda's smile lit up her porcelain-fine features. "Wonderful. You've got to see them before you leave again for that godforsaken island of yours. They started school this year, you know."

"School?" Jack stared at her. Wasn't it only yesterday that he had sat with Belinda and Frenchie by the pool in their backyard, watching their two red-haired toddlers run stiff-legged across the grass? Yet now the twins were in school, Frenchie was gone and everything had changed. Time was getting the better of him.

"Jamie looks more like Frenchie every day. And he's turning into as much of a daredevil as his father was."

"I'll come by to see them," Jack said resolutely, as though steeling himself. "As soon as I can get away."

Belinda nodded, glanced at her cigarette, then suddenly stubbed it out. "Jack," she began, her voice serious, "what are you really doing here? It isn't just to see me and the twins, is it?"

He pretended offense, then sighed. "Not entirely," he admitted reluctantly. "Though you were first on my list."

"So, what are you doing in Las Vegas?" Belinda persisted.

He tried to look innocent. "Nothing special. I've had a few, well, financial setbacks. With the resort. The old governor's mansion is like a mausoleum. It sat empty for more than a dozen years, you know. Unfortunately, the renovations are costing more than I'd counted on."

"You've gotten back into it," she stated simply, a thread of regret in her voice. "That's why you're here."

Jack slugged back the last of his whiskey and didn't reply.

"You said you were finished with all of that," Belinda went on. "After Frenchie died, you told me that you weren't ever getting back into the business again. You said you'd promised yourself that it was your last job."

Unable to look at her, Jack lit a cigarette he didn't really want, knowing that Belinda's disappointment in him was at least partially justified. He *had* made those promises to himself. At the time, he'd meant to keep them. But that was before he'd realized how much copper-plated pipes, electrical rewiring, Italian marble and silk wallpaper cost when the place you required them in was an out-of-the-way island in the Bahamas. The expense of finding *and* keeping skilled labor, alone, was almost breaking him.

The stark truth, which he would never have confided to Belinda, was that he was nearly broke. If he didn't manage to increase the little capital he had left—and increase it fast—there would be no further renovations. And that was something he could never allow. He'd dreamed about owning his own resort for too many years. He'd put too much of himself into it. If he failed now, just when he was so close to success . . .

"I'm not getting back into anything," Jack said unconvincingly. "Those days are over. I meant it when I said I was getting out. I'm just doing a little recreational gambling."

"You're up to something," Belinda insisted. "You've come back to pull a job, haven't you?"

Jack thought of the red-faced, vulgar-mouthed Texan he'd been playing poker with at the Sunburst's private tables. He'd left the man sitting happily behind a growing mound of thousand-dollar chips, getting more and more self-confident by the minute and ripening nicely for the final play.

"No, I haven't. This time I'm here completely on the up-and-up. I have some capital left. That's all. I'm just trying to increase it at the tables."

The corners of Belinda's mouth drooped, and she looked sad. "I wish I believed you."

"It's the truth." Jack frowned. Belinda knew him too well.

With a deep sigh, he finally relented. "Okay. All right, you win. Maybe there *is* a mark or two I might string along for a while. There are a couple of cocky punters over at the Sunburst who might feel a small pinch in their wallets—well-deserved, mind you. But that's it. That's all I'm doing. I promise you."

Belinda studied him with doubtful eyes. "You know, I don't see many of Frenchie's old acquaintances anymore. But I still hear things, Jack. From time to time, I hear rumors."

"Rumors?" He frowned, alert. "What sort of rumors?"

"Not a rumor, really. More of a whisper." Belinda shifted in her chair, glancing around so quickly and so nonchalantly that no one but Jack would ever have detected the movement. "I heard that there was something going down this weekend. Something *really* big. Maybe with one of the casinos."

"And then you heard that I was back in town." Jack smiled softly and reached for Belinda's hand. "It's not me. I swear it."

"Jack, after what happened to Frenchie—"

"It's *not* me. I promise you, I'm not involved in anything like that. Never again. You don't need to worry. Nothing's going to happen to me."

Belinda nodded warily. "All right. But just be careful, Jack. Please. I couldn't bear to lose both my husband and my favorite cousin. I couldn't."

"I'm always careful. You know that." Reassuringly, Jack squeezed her hand. "So, tell me what you've been up to lately. Did you finally agree to go to dinner with that lawyer from Aspen? Or are you still tormenting the poor guy?"

Sydney sat on the edge of the narrow bed in her hotel room and held the receiver well away from her ear. Even from that distance, she could hear Sheila's breathless, frenzied chatter. Reaching for the can of diet soda on the nightstand, she flipped open the tab, poured the drink into a glass over ice and sipped it, waiting for a break in her older sister's ravings.

The blackmailer's phone call at a quarter after midnight had shaken Sydney, although she didn't tell Sheila that. His latest demand *was* an unexpected and potentially disastrous development, and although she knew that it was Sheila's own stupidity that had gotten her into this mess, Sydney still felt sorry for her.

That was the most ironic thing about their relationship, Sydney realized. Beautiful, golden-haired, popular Sheila was the last person anyone would think needed sympathy, especially sympathy from a drab, nearsighted, unsuccessful bumbler like herself. Yet, it had always been Sheila—Sheila

with the dates, the gorgeous figure and the lucky breaks—
who had run to fat lonely Sydney with her tales of woe.
Never the other way around.

She had stopped feeling envious of Sheila a long time ago,
about the same time she had finally accepted her own dull
looks—and, in fact, had learned to use them to her own ad-
vantage. Even when her parents exhorted her to try to be
more like Sheila, without bothering to hide their disappointment in Sydney, she knew she'd rather be boiled in hot
oil than comply.

Maybe she wasn't much to look at and maybe she did
slave away at a dead-end job, but she liked the freedom she
had to take photographs during the day before her shift began, and she liked the self-sufficiency she gained by earn-
ing her own living. What was more, at least she'd never been
naive—or vain—enough to believe some joker could make
her a star if only she took her clothes off and let him take
pictures of her. Not that the question had ever arisen.

"...will ruin him, Syd. Absolutely ruin him. Ambrose will
divorce me. Of course he'll divorce me. And the campaign—oh, Syd—all the work. All the *money*. My God,
what am I going to do?"

Sydney set her glass on the nightstand and cleared her
throat. "The first thing to do is *stop* panicking." Even as she
said it, she realized her advice was a little late. "Just calm
down, and let's think about this. Are you sure you don't
have any more money in your account?"

Sheila was uncharacteristically silent.

"Sheila, can you get hold of any more cash?"

"Well, no. Not really."

"Sheila," Sydney said sternly.

"Maybe just a little, tiny bit more. But I need it, Syd.
How can I show up at campaign dinners in the same old
thing, night after night. It's...it's a business expense."

"Sheila. Listen to me. If you don't get your hands on another five thousand dollars, there isn't going to *be* a campaign."

She could sense her sister pouting at the end of the line.

"I don't see why he wants five thousand dollars more. He should be lucky we even agreed to ten thousand. Can't you make him stick to our original bargain? Can't you talk to him?"

Sydney sighed. "Listen to me, Sheila. You sent me here to take care of this for you, and I'm doing the best I can. Can't you understand? This guy is a sleezeball, and he knows he's sitting in the driver's seat. He isn't about to bargain with us. I mean, how much do you think a tabloid would dole out to him for those pictures? Plenty, I'd guess. Think about it. Your bare butt plastered across every newsstand and every grocery-store magazine rack in America."

"Oh, my God, Syd—"

"Obviously, this guy doesn't care whether you have anything to wear to the Royal Moose Lodge dinner or not. He's out to get the most he can for those pictures. If we don't give it to him, he knows that someone else will. And he knows we know that." Sydney paused wearily. "I'm telling you, it was a mistake, Sheila. You should have gone to the police straightaway. They would have caught this guy and locked him up weeks ago."

"No!" Sheila's cry was a little hysterical. "That would mean a trial. Publicity. You said so yourself. Ambrose's campaign would be ruined. No one would vote for him, and then I'd never get to Washington."

With difficulty, Sydney swallowed a retort, and merely breathed deeply. "Then I don't see that you have too many other choices. You're going to have to pay him what he's asking. How much more can you scrape together?"

"I think . . . Wait." A rustling came over the phone, then Sheila said weakly, "A thousand-two hundred."

"What?"

"There's only a thousand-two hundred in my account. It's all I've got left." Sheila whimpered. "That's it. I'm ruined. He's won. My whole life is ruined. Ambrose will find out what I did. He'll never forgive . . ."

Sydney stopped listening as she stared across the room. The leather case with her beloved camera sat on the dresser where she'd dumped it after her afternoon on the Strip. A momentary, stinging sense of inevitable defeat, of bitter but not wholly unexpected loss, overcame her as she gazed at her precious equipment. Then she realized that, even if she pawned it, they still wouldn't have enough money to meet the blackmailer's new demands.

If only she were Clint Eastwood, Sydney thought. She'd tear this guy limb from limb and make sure he never terrorized her sister again.

"Look," Sydney interrupted her sister's long description of the horrors of divorce. "I already told you that you should confess everything to Ambrose. The whole stupid fiasco happened a long time ago, and you were young and...and innocent. He'd understand. He is your husband, after all."

Sydney thought briefly of her too-friendly, overly confident brother-in-law, who reminded her of an ambitious used-car salesman. She tried to imagine his reaction when he was told that his senate campaign was doomed because his wife had posed for nude photographs in her youth. The image was too horrible for words.

"Well, anyway, there's no reason for him to find out, Sheila. He doesn't ever have to know anything about this."

"But the *money*. I don't have any more money."

Sydney glanced at her camera case again, then looked away. "We'll think of something. The creep's given us three days. We'll come up with an idea by then."

"Oh, Syd. Will we? Will we really?"

Sydney squeezed her eyes shut against the misery in her sister's voice. "Sure we will," she said with all the conviction she could muster. "I've never let you down before, have I? I'll think of something, Sheila. I will. I promise."

* * *

In a motel room on the other side of town, a beautiful woman of indeterminate age was throwing a violent tantrum.

"You damned, stupid idiot!" Rachel Bennet hurled her Gucci purse against the wall and glowered in fury at her lover. "How could you be so pathetically stupid?"

Unhappily, Tony Martin hunched in his chair, worry clouding his perfect, though vacant, features. On the table before him sat a disposable container in which his half-eaten breakfast was rapidly congealing. Wistfully, he gave the food a hungry look and heard his stomach growl in protest. Yet he didn't dare take another bite of the barely tasted egg and sausage sandwich.

"I'm sorry, Rachel," he mumbled. "But I didn't lose the key. I swear, I—"

"Sorry?" she shrieked, and was off again, her tirade seeming to have doubled in strength.

Tony slumped, miserable and confused. He wished he wasn't hiding out in this dirty motel room. He wished Rachel would understand he'd done his best. He even wished he was back at his job at the Sunburst, making his presence felt along with the other hired muscle. He'd never really minded the job, and Mr. Van Hausen had always been good to him. Of course, the old guy hadn't known that Tony was sleeping with his mistress and planning to rob him.

Cringing as Rachel called him a particularly foul name, Tony wished briefly that he'd never gotten involved with her. But that thought skated too close to disloyalty, and quickly, mentally, he took it back.

Rachel was everything to him, wasn't she? Why, hadn't she planned it all? Hadn't she shown him just what to do? Without her, he would be just another flunky—another faceless soldier in Mr. Van Hausen's private army, as Rachel liked to say. She was going to change his life. Together, they were going places. He was going to be somebody, and all because of Rachel.

Still, he didn't like it when she got so angry with him. Silently, he watched her sweep everything off the desk with one furious swipe of her arm. He followed the path of an ashtray as it spun around on the worn carpet, finally coming to rest under his chair.

"Someone was following me, Rachel," he finally said during a break in her shouting. "Somehow, Mr. V. found out. Or I was spotted. I don't know. But someone was following me. I got scared. Really scared. How would it look if they caught me with all that money on me? I had to get rid of it."

Standing in the middle of the shabby room with her hands on her hips, Rachel glared at him, her eyes narrowed with scorn. "You're so damned stupid. Weak and stupid. No one was following you, Tony. *No one*. You should have brought the money back here, just as we planned. Instead, you stashed it in a bus locker. I mean, a *bus* locker!"

"I'm telling you, Rachel, there was someone—"

Throwing up her hands in a gesture of disgust, Rachel snarled, "My God, I can't believe this. I can't believe this is really happening. All the work I've done. The sacrifices I've made. How I planned and waited for just the right moment. And *you* put the money in a damned locker and lose the key."

"I was scared, Rachel. I told you, I—"

"Shut up!"

Ducking the cheap plastic ice bucket she threw at him, Tony obeyed.

"You idiot," Rachel muttered as she lowered herself to the edge of the bed, careful to smooth the expensive fabric of her Lacroix suit before sitting down. "Do you realize what you've done? Do you realize what could happen to us—to *both* of us—unless we find that key? Without the key, we can't get the money out of that locker. And without the money, there's no way for us to get out of this city."

"But that's what I've been trying to tell—"

"Believe me," Rachel continued, unheeding, "Carlton isn't going to stop until he finds the person who took his money. And every day he looks, Tony, he's going to get closer and closer until he figures out what's been going on between us. Once he does that, he's not going to have to think very hard to put the rest of the story together."

"We've been careful," Tony insisted ineffectually.

"If we don't get that money back and get away soon," Rachel went on, ignoring him, "then you and I, Tony, are going to be very dead."

Dry-mouthed, Tony stared at the carpet.

Suddenly, Rachel sprang to her feet and turned on him, her beautiful tawny eyes flashing like a tigress. "Well, *I* am not going to sit around waiting for Carlton to kill me. That filthy, nasty old man with his cold hands—he's seen the last of Rachel Bennet. You're going to find that key, Tony. You're going to find the key to that locker and get that money out."

"But I *didn't* lose it. I swear I didn't," Tony moaned. "That's what I keep trying to tell you. I sent the key to your suite. Then I came here. I've been waiting for you ever since."

"If you sent the key to my suite," Rachel hissed, "how come I don't have it?"

Blankly, Tony stared at her.

"I'll tell you why," Rachel continued, her teeth clenched. "Because you never sent it."

"I did. I swear I did."

"Then where is it?"

Tony ran a hand through his thick, sun-bleached hair and thought hard, harder than he'd thought in a very long time.

"Where, Tony?"

"I don't know, Rachel. I swear to God. I don't know. I wrote your suite number on—" He broke off, confusion playing over his face.

Rachel stopped pacing and almost pounced on him. "What? What?" she cried shrilly.

"I put your suite number on the envelope. No names. Just like we always do. Maybe I wrote the wrong number."

Rachel looked up at the ceiling, breathing hard. "What number did you put on the envelope?" she asked, her voice strained. "Think carefully. What number did you write?"

"Number 1203."

"That *is* my suite. That's not a wrong number. Think, Tony. Are you sure that's the number you wrote on the envelope?"

Tony bit his lip, then suddenly widened his eyes. "I was scared. Really freaked-out. Maybe I wrote 203. Yes, I think I got mixed up. I think I wrote 203."

Rachel straightened, her hard, beautiful face suddenly triumphant. "So all we have to do is get that key back from the person staying in 203."

"Yes," Tony agreed meekly.

"You can do that tonight. Whoever's staying in that room will probably be in the casino most of the evening."

"All right."

"You understand that you've got to come back to work today, don't you? You can't hide out in this dump any longer. Carlton's due in from Atlantic City this afternoon. If you're gone, he's not going to look any farther for the money than you."

White-faced, Tony stared at her. "Rachel, I can't. He'll look at me with those eyes of his." He shuddered. "He'll know in a minute. He always knows everything."

"Then you'll just have to stay out of his way. You'll be at the casino, but we'll make sure you're too busy to see him right away. He won't know a thing. But you've *got* to go back to work. Everyone will know if you don't."

"Please, Rachel—"

"He'll know it was you."

"Okay." Tony inhaled deeply. "Okay. You're right."

"Good." As quickly as Rachel's anger had come, it disappeared. It was always that way. She smiled at him now, as though nothing had ever been wrong. "I'm so glad we have everything settled."

Stepping forward, she inched the skirt of her suit slowly higher up her thighs and straddled his outstretched legs. "We have a few hours... before we need to leave. Don't we?"

This was what he'd been hoping for when she'd first arrived this morning, before she'd started screaming at him. Still nervous, Tony slid a hand against her smooth, silky thigh. Things were going to be okay now, he thought dully.

"Sure, Rachel," he replied as she rubbed against him. "Sure, we have a few hours."

"Of course we do, darling," she purred. "What would Rachel do without her Tony-doll?"

With sweaty palms, Sydney stood anxiously outside a closed door in a hushed corridor of the Sunburst Casino and Hotel. She'd been awake since five-thirty that morning, mulling over the idea that had come to her in her sleep. Over and over, she'd considered every possibility until she'd convinced herself that it really wasn't as risky as it seemed.

Finally, at eight o'clock, she couldn't sit in her tiny room any longer and she'd taken the elevator to the tenth floor. Yet now that she was actually here—about to put Sheila's whole future on the line—she wondered what could have possessed her. What if he was asleep? What if he wouldn't help her? What if—good heavens!—what if he wasn't alone?

Sydney thought of the beautiful blonde from the bar and started to turn away. She'd only knocked once softly, and no one had come to the door yet. There was still time to turn tail and run. There was no reason she had to go through with—

"Yes?"

In the open doorway stood an enormous man, gazing at her expectantly. Large and towering, he was wearing an enormous white linen suit and his head was as bald as a boiled egg. Despite his menacing appearance, his brown eyes were soft, like a cocker spaniel's.

"Oh. I must have the wrong room." Sydney fumbled with her purse and scanned the creased white card. "I was looking for Mr. Ames. Mr. Jack Ames."

"He's here," the giant said simply. His voice was low and gravelly and his words indistinct, as if he were speaking around a mouthful of marbles.

"He is?"

"Yeah. He's asleep."

"Oh. Well, in that case, maybe I'll just try again later. If you could tell him Syd Stone stopped by. No need to disturb—"

A giant hand closed around her elbow. Unable to resist, Sydney felt herself being gently eased through the doorway.

"That's okay. He sleeps too much," the big man said, propelling her into the room. "I'm Claus. I work for Mr. Ames."

"Yeah? Really?" Sydney blathered nervously. "My name's Syd...I mean, Sydney Stone. I didn't know he— Wow!"

Amazed, Sydney stopped dead in her tracks and looked around her. "Wow," she breathed again.

"Pretty nice, huh?"

"It's fantastic. I didn't know they had rooms like this."

"It's a suite. Mr. Ames always stays here when we come to Vegas. You want some breakfast?"

"What?" Awed, Sydney gazed across the three tiers of snow-white carpeting that descended to a balcony and a magnificent view of the city. Chairs and sofas in peach-colored fabric were clustered in tasteful groups, and a startling statue of a satyr in pale blue marble stood near a white baby grand piano.

"Breakfast," Claus repeated. "I could make you my specialty. Raspberry crepes."

"Make?" Sydney turned to him. "There's a *kitchen?*"

"Sure. We've got everything. You want me to make you some?"

"No, thanks. I'm not very hungry." At the expression of disappointment that crossed his broad face, Sydney added, "A cup of coffee maybe?"

"Sure," Claus said, instantly cheered. "I'll grind some beans. You like mocha?"

"Yeah. Great." Slightly bewildered, Sydney watched him lumber enthusiastically past an elegant glass-topped dining table, complete with twelve chairs, and head toward a door. "Do you mind if I look around?" she called.

"Help yourself."

Alone, Sydney wandered down to the second tier and sat in a cushioned chair, sinking deeply into its satiny depths. Next, she strolled to the piano and ran her fingers over the keys. What a spread, she thought in amazement. Now she knew what you could get if you paid more than nineteen ninety-five for a room in this place.

By the time she heard a door open and Claus call her name, she felt as though she'd stumbled on to an episode of "Lifestyles of The Rich and Famous." She could almost hear Robin Leach's refined tones describing everything as she graciously showed him around "her" suite.

"Holy cow!" she exclaimed, returning to the living room. "The bathroom's as big as my whole mobile home. You could throw a party just in the shower—"

Startled, Sydney halted. Claus was calmly laying out cups and saucers on a low table, and behind him, Jack Ames stood scowling at her.

"Do you realize that it's eight-thirty in the morning?" he demanded indignantly. His precise, faintly refined voice, which had so impressed her last night, now lent an added coolness to his words.

Stricken, Sydney swallowed hard. "I'm sorry. Maybe I better go."

"I'm making her a coffee," Claus said in his low mumble. Without glancing at either of them, he lifted a silver pot and poured coffee into a cup.

"That's not what I asked." Annoyed, Jack ran a hand through his hair.

"You said she was an interesting girl," Claus said, moving the sugar bowl to just the right spot. When he straightened up, he smiled at Sydney and nodded invitingly toward the table he'd laid out.

Jack looked baffled. "I did *not* say 'girl,' Claus. I never say 'girl.' You should learn what's politically correct. I said 'young woman.'"

"Cream and sugar?" Claus asked her, ignoring his employer.

Sydney stared from one man to the other. "I think I'll just go and come back later."

"But your coffee's ready."

"Oh, hell," Jack grumbled, throwing himself onto a sofa and covering his eyes with a hand. "Stay and drink your coffee. That is, unless you want me to get the silent treatment for the rest of the day."

The delicate cup and saucer Claus extended to her was almost lost in his large hand. "I got to finish peeling shrimp," he said and abruptly turned away to plod toward the kitchen.

For a long moment, Sydney just stood there, holding her coffee awkwardly and staring at Jack Ames's inert form on the sofa. Pajama bottoms and slippers stuck out from the hem of his silk robe, but his lapels had fallen open and she could see a broad, bare, muscular chest sprinkled with black curling hairs. The utter, complete masculinity of those hard, dark lines made her throat tighten. Despite her best efforts, she couldn't seem to look away.

After silently watching him for a while, she began to wonder if he might have gone back to sleep. Finally, she ventured, "I'm sorry I bothered you this early in the morning."

She heard a muffled grunt from the sofa.

"It's just that I didn't know what else to do. The only person I could think of was you." With a deep breath, Sydney blurted out, "I need you."

# 3

$$\longrightarrow \bullet \longleftarrow$$

Slowly, Jack swung his legs off the sofa and gazed at her. Sydney noticed he looked tired, more tired than he had the night before.

"You need me?"

"Yes . . . Well, no. I mean, I need your help. You see, I'm . . . I'm . . ." The words stuck in her throat. Blushing furiously, she finally blurted out, "I'm being blackmailed."

Expressionlessly, Jack studied her, then reached for the silver coffeepot and poured himself a cup. Slumping back against the cushions with the cup and saucer resting against his chest, he regarded her silently.

"I see," he said at last. "This wouldn't have anything to do with that letter you showed me or our meeting last night, would it?"

"Oh, no. That was just coincidence."

Still eyeing her without a flicker of emotion, he seemed to be thinking. "You'd better sit down," he finally said. When she was seated, balancing her cup on her knees, he raised his head and shouted, "Claus! I need something stronger than coffee."

A huge, shining pate appeared around the edge of the door beyond the glass dining table. "You drank too much already last night," Claus grumbled, then disappeared.

Wearily, Jack looked down at his coffee, then took a sip. "Maybe you should tell me about it," he said, setting his cup down and massaging his temples.

"All right." Sydney cleared her throat. "You said that you could double my money for me. Well, I want you to do that."

Jack paused. "I said I could *try.*"

"Okay. Then I want you to try."

"I don't know," he said. "I don't know if that would be right."

"I don't have any other choice." For a split second, Sydney heard an echo of her sister's panic in her own voice. Taking a deep breath, she added more calmly, "He wants another five thousand dollars and I don't have it."

Jack lowered his hands and looked at her, concern in his eyes. "Why is someone blackmailing you, Sydney?"

"Do you have to know that?"

"If I'm going to be involved—mind you, I said *if*—then yes, I think I should know that."

"I was afraid you might say that." With a hand that was trembling ever so slightly, Sydney set her cup on the table, wiped her damp palms on her skirt and recited the story she'd come up with—a story which was, unfortunately, a little too close to the truth.

"A few years ago, when I first left home to be on my own, I met someone. A guy. I wanted to be an actress then, and he said he could help me if—"

Lifting a hand to stop her, Jack closed his eyes. "If you let him take pictures of you," he finished for her regretfully, as though it was a tale he'd heard a thousand times. He sighed. "Son of a bitch. I hate that kind of slime bag."

Sydney bit her lip. "Will you help me?"

Wordlessly, he considered her, then reached behind the sofa to fumble with a cigarette case on the table behind him. Still watching her, he lit a cigarette.

"What makes you think you can trust *me?*" he asked, blowing smoke out in a long stream.

"Because I can. I know I can. I knew it the first time I saw you." As soon as she said it, she knew it was true. Hadn't she read in *Cosmopolitan* magazine that a person's first impressions were almost always right? Or had she seen that in *Ladies' Home Journal?*

One dark eyebrow rose a fraction. "You don't know anything about me."

"No, I don't," she agreed. "Do I need to?"

He sighed and gave a small smile. "No. No, I guess not."

"So, you'll help me?"

"Yes," he said, not sounding too pleased. "I'll help."

Beaming, Sydney leaned back in her chair, relaxing for the first time since entering the suite. "Thanks. Thank you so much. You'll never know what this means to me."

"I already know. It means five thousand dollars."

Sydney shook her head. "No. More than that. A lot more."

A faint smile touched his lips. "Don't be too grateful yet. We still have to win, you know."

"I know. When can we start?"

In the act of stubbing out his cigarette, he paused abruptly to turn to her. "We?"

"Yes. Us."

"Wait a minute. You asked me to help you, and I've agreed. But I'm going to do things my way. I'll put your share in with mine and give you a cut of the profits from the night."

Sydney nodded, although she wasn't sure she completely followed him. "Okay. That sounds good. Can we start tonight?"

Jack frowned. "I don't think you understand. I don't gamble downstairs on the casino floor, Sydney."

"You don't?"

"No. The house doesn't generally cover the kind of stakes I play with. They'll only do that for private games. I play at specially arranged tables for invited guests."

"Oh." A little deflated, Sydney felt her smile fade. "You mean, I'm not invited."

"Well, in all honesty, no."

"But you could take me with you."

His frown deepened. "I don't think—"

"You could, couldn't you?"

"Yes, I suppose so, but—"

Sydney straightened her shoulders. "You're going to have ten thousand dollars of *my* money. Now, I know that doesn't sound like a lot to a big shot like yourself, but it happens to be all the money I have." She paused, and her eyes narrowed as a sudden, almost painful thought occurred to her. "Or is it that you're afraid I might embarrass you?"

Jack looked distinctly uncomfortable. "You must admit, you present a, well, a... different appearance. Not exactly the sort of look that you generally see at these events. You might feel uncomfortable with the kind of people— Hey, wait a minute. What are you doing? Where are you going? Sydney! Ah, hell." Scowling, Jack scrambled to his feet, calling after her retreating figure, "All right, you can come with me. Sydney? I said you could come with me. Sydney?"

Throwing up his hands in frustration, Jack shouted, "Claus!"

"I don't know," Claus shook his head as he looked over the dress. "This isn't going to work, either."

From the bed in her hotel room, Sydney watched Claus's huge hands pick another dress from her closet. He held it up and studied it critically. "No. We got to do something about this."

Sydney rolled her eyes, still annoyed. Jack's parting words to Claus had been "Fix her up or something before tonight." The memory of the way her cheeks had burned made her fume anew. She had wanted to tell him to forget it, that she wasn't going *anywhere* with him. But Jack had already retreated and shut his bedroom door with a firm, deliberate click before she'd calmed down enough to speak.

"I'll tell you what," Claus said. "I got an idea."

"Those are all the clothes I have." Sydney sniffed angrily and picked at the cheap cotton bedspread. "And there's not a thing wrong with any of them."

"Except that they're all too big for you. Why do you want to wear clothes this big?"

"Because I used to *be* that big," she snapped. Springing to her feet, she snatched the dress from him and hung it up.

"You?" Claus asked innocently. He glanced back in surprise at the few dresses hanging limply in the closet.

"Yeah, me. Oh, this is ridiculous. Let's just forget this whole thing."

Claus shook his massive head. "Can't do that, Miss Sydney. You're going with Mr. Ames tonight." He watched her with his slow but friendly gaze. "You're just embarrassed. That's all. Wait till you see what Claus has planned." He tapped his shiny scalp meaningfully.

"I don't think I like the sound of that," Sydney muttered.

"You will." He stepped back and examined her. "You'll like it."

Squirming under his scrutiny, Sydney cast around for anything to change the subject from her deficiencies in the glamor department. "So, Claus. Have you been with Jack for a long time?"

Occupied with his considerations, he nodded. "Sure. A long time."

"Really?"

Putting a large finger under her chin, he turned her face to the side. "Ever since he won me. In Monte Carlo."

"Ever since he what?" Sydney stared up at him. "That's horrible. He *won* you? That's the worst thing I've ever heard. It's awful."

"No, it's not. I like Mr. Ames. The other guy wasn't so nice. He always ate out. Do you have contact lenses?"

"Do you *have* to work for him? I mean, you can leave if you want, can't you?"

"Sure. But why would I want to? I'm going to be the pastry chef when Mr. Ames opens his resort."

Sydney gazed at him blankly. "You are?"

"Contacts would be good. Do you have some?"

"Yeah. Somewhere. But I never wear them. I don't— Hey, wait a minute," she cried as a big hand lifted her glasses off her face. "I can't see anything without those, Claus."

"You can put your contacts in."

"They make my eyes itch."

"No pain, no gain," Claus said philosophically.

"*Really* itch," she insisted.

"Miss Sydney."

Gritting her teeth in frustration, Sydney reached blindly for her purse. "I'm starting to see why Jack sighs all the time around you."

At the windows of his penthouse office, Carlton Van Hausen stood behind the delicately carved Sheraton desk, his hands clasped behind his back. Fury made his cold, immobile face more rigid still. Across the room, lounging in feline sleekness, his mistress Rachel Bennet watched him with her wide golden eyes. God, she was a tiger, that one, Carlton thought. And he'd been looking forward to spending his first night back from Atlantic City with her.

Instead, he had a thief to catch.

"I'm not saying it means anything," his business manager, Frank Bovo said. "But nobody thought he was too flush anymore. And he has been flashing around an awful lot of cash."

Van Hausen stared fixedly out the window without speaking. Behind him, he heard Bovo fidget nervously. Apparently, he'd spotted the safe in the wall, which Van Hausen had purposely left open, gaping and empty. Good, Van Hausen thought in a rage. Let him stew. He should have been keeping an eye on things. That's what he got paid for.

"If you want," Bovo continued shakily, "I could have a couple of the boys interview him. See if he knows anything about this."

Slowly, Van Hausen turned, and one glance from his cold steel gray eyes was enough to silence the man.

"Don't be a complete fool," Van Hausen snapped. "Even if Jack wasn't an old friend of mine, he wouldn't be stupid enough to steal two million dollars from me, then continue to stay at my hotel."

"I don't know," Bovo said, wetting his lips. "If you ask me, it sounds just like the kind of thing he'd do."

For a brief instant, Van Hausen's hard, chiseled mouth twitched in something that could almost be called a smile. "Maybe," he said. "Maybe."

"I think we should talk to him, sir."

Van Hausen turned back to the window and considered the situation. He and Jack Ames went back a long way. He'd known Jack from the early days, when he was still busting his ass trying to get his casino started and Jack was rolling in dough from his elaborate con games and European jewel heists. They'd had some good laughs together back then.

Yet, things changed. He'd always known Jack didn't have what it took to make it big. Really big. He'd never been smart—or did he mean ruthless?—enough to watch his own back.

Just look at how their roles had reversed. Jack was scraping the bottom of the barrel putting that ridiculous resort together on San Miguel, and he . . . Well, he was living in a penthouse with the most luscious dancer to have ever stepped foot on a Vegas stage. Yes, if Jack was flashing around a lot of cash, it was surprising.

"All right," Van Hausen said icily. "Have a talk with him."

"Right. I'll get on it right away," Bovo said quickly, anxious to leave the office.

"One thing," Van Hausen called after his manager, just before the man could shut the door. With a finger raised warningly, he cautioned with predatory softness, "Not his face, Bovo. Jack makes his living off his face. And after all, he *is* an old friend."

"Yes, sir."

As Bovo shut the door, Van Hausen turned to Rachel. "I've been neglecting you, my dear. If I can get away from all this, what would you like to do tonight? Dinner? Dancing? Anything you like."

With a dazzling smile, Rachel gave a catlike stretch and reached for his hand.

"Are you ready?" Claus called in his deep, fumbling voice.

"Yes, yes. I'm ready," Jack grumbled.

Having dressed in a black tuxedo an hour earlier, he was scowling impatiently, his thoughts already at the gambling table he would soon be joining and the winnings he hoped to take away with him this evening. Not enough to finish the renovations on the resort, but a good start. Tonight, he could definitely make a healthy increase in his capital. If they ever got out of the suite.

"For heaven's sake, Claus," Jack barked. "Just bring her out so we can go."

"Close your eyes."

"I am *not* going to close my eyes, Claus. For the last time, it's getting late. So, if you don't..." Jack's words faded away, and he realized he was gaping, his mouth open in astonishment.

"What do you think?" Claus rumbled happily.

Speechlessly, Jack stared at the young woman Claus led out of the guest bedroom.

"She's gorgeous, yes?"

"Sydney?" Jack asked, taken back.

Anxiously, she glanced at Claus. When the big man grinned and waved a hand, Jack saw her breathe deeply, then turn slowly around in precariously slender high heels. Her hair, which he'd never really noticed before, fell halfway down her back in soft, shining golden waves. Her large, owl-like glasses had gone, revealing wide, startlingly blue eyes and delicate, high cheekbones. Gone, too, were the cotton sacks she used to wear. The straight, simple gown of midnight blue satin, strapless and slit from ankle to knee, gave him plenty of clues about what those sacks had hidden.

She was gorgeous. Stunning. If he hadn't seen it with his own two eyes, Jack thought, he would never have believed it possible. Sydney Stone was a knockout with enough curves to turn the head of any man alive.

"She looks fantastic," he told Claus.

"Good," the giant said. "Because we used your credit cards."

Jack barely heard him. "What? Oh, yes. Fine. That's fine."

Unable to tear his gaze away, he stared at Sydney. Her hair caught the light like fine-spun gold, and he had a sudden urge to touch the wispy mass of gossamer curls, tangle his fingers in it and feel the silkiness between his fingers.

How had he ever thought her unattractive? He must have been blind. Warm and round, downy-soft like a ripe peach, she made his most masculine desires rise to the surface. Unconsciously, he straightened to his full height, swelling his chest.

"I'm too fat," Sydney said, watching him closely for his reaction.

"Fat?" Jack turned to Claus again in disbelief. "Is she kidding?"

Claus shrugged. "I tried to tell her. Guys don't like skinny women. But she won't listen. Reads too many women's magazines."

"Sydney," Jack said, trying to ignore the stirring in his groin at the sight of the milky-white curves and dark cleavage above her dress. "You aren't fat. That's definitely not the word that springs to mind."

"Yeah. Sexy springs to mind. Right, Mr. Ames?"

Jack glowered at him. "Don't you have something to do in the kitchen, Claus?"

"No."

Jack narrowed his eyes. "I think I hear something boiling over."

Claus blinked. "Boiling ov— Oh, you want me to leave. Okay." Flicking his hand under Sydney's chin so that she almost toppled over, the big man grinned. "Have a good time tonight, Miss Sydney."

When he had gone, Sydney gave Jack a doubtful look. "You really think I look okay?"

Jack wondered how she could even ask. Could she honestly not know?

"I feel stupid," she said.

Speechlessly, Jack watched her cross the room.

With slow, careful steps that he knew were caused by her high heels but which looked like a graceful, seductive dance, she sat uneasily on the edge of a chair and looked up at him with clear, guileless blue eyes. Had he ever seen a more beautiful, more heart-stopping pair of eyes? Had he ever known a woman with a more translucent, candid gaze, as though he could see straight through to her soul?

Maybe her involvement with those nude pictures was a little more understandable now, but only a little. Somehow, he still didn't wholly believe in her story. She was certainly built like a pinup model, but something still bothered him. Maybe, he suddenly thought, it was what he saw in her eyes—or what he didn't.

Self-consciously now, she fiddled with her small satin handbag, turning it this way and that and looking anywhere but at him.

"Sydney," Jack began, then stopped. He cupped a hand over his chin and scrutinized her. "I'm . . . I'm impressed."

"Yeah?" Her voice carried a strain of false bravado. "Big change, huh?"

"Well, yes." He frowned slightly at her tone. "I can't believe it. You look marvelous."

"Thanks," she said, not sounding thankful at all.

"I mean it. Really."

Finally, she glanced at him. "Well, don't get too excited. Remember, under this flashy getup and all this paint is still the same old, fat Syd who slings hash for a living." Despite her carefully light voice, he caught the glimmer of a shadow in her blue eyes. His gut tightened.

"Sydney—"

"So. Let's get out of here," she said briskly, rising suddenly. "You've been hollering for the last half hour about how late we are."

Jack hesitated, sensing that something wasn't quite right and that he should say something. He wasn't exactly sure what was wrong, so he nodded at her, then said, "All right. Do you remember everything I told you? We're playing poker tonight, and not against the house. There'll be two Texans at our table. Ryle Jamison is the one we're concentrating on. He's—"

"A stubby, red-faced guy with a big mouth. Yeah, I remember."

"Good." He wanted to take her arm, but she brushed by him and toward the door, leaving him to follow behind. "Most of the women will be playing roulette or blackjack. Some of them will be watching their dates play poker. That's what I want you—"

"Just dates?" Sydney asked, tripping as they neared the door.

Quickly, he gripped her wrist, not at all surprised at the softness of her skin under his fingers before she righted herself and pulled away.

"I mean," she continued, "aren't wives allowed?"

"Well, yes. Of course they are. But you'll hardly ever meet one at these gatherings."

"Why not?"

He opened the door, not sure whether she was seriously asking him or just teasing. "Because, Sydney, I was using the word *date* euphemistically."

"Using it what?"

"In it's broadest possible sense." He caught her puzzled look and decided to just spell it out. "A lot of the women you'll meet tonight are being paid."

Her blue eyes widened. "Oh, I get it."

He held her arm again as they walked down the hall toward the elevator, savoring the velvety softness of her skin under his fingers. When the elevator doors opened, revealing several other passengers, she pulled away once more.

On the ride up, he could feel her watching him, her gaze glued to his face. Finally, he looked down at her.

"What is it?" he asked gently, nodding in polite recognition across the elevator at a black-suited Venezuelan he'd often seen around the tables.

"Do you think everyone will think," she whispered back, "that I'm, well, you know... Also."

"Also what?"

"*You know.*" Her whisper was fierce, as though she was willing him to read her mind. "That you're, you know, paying."

Realization dawned on him, and Jack grinned. "No, Sydney. You're much too bossy. No one will think I'd throw good money away on such—Ouch!"

Bending down to rub his shin, he caught her innocent smile, directed at the other, staring passengers.

All day long, a low-burning anger had simmered in Sydney. It wasn't that she minded playing dress up. In fact, it had been fun, and she'd been pleasantly stunned when she'd seen the results of all the work put in by the hotel's salon and boutique. Yet she felt that she was only playacting, pretending to be someone she wasn't, and that made the appreciative reactions of everyone she met all the harder to take.

People liked the fake Sydney much better than the real one.

What hurt most of all was Jack's response. She'd seen the surprise on his face, followed by that look of approval, as though he was seeing her for the first time. And that, she had decided, was probably the real problem. He *was* seeing her for the first time. He'd never really noticed her before.

As they walked down the long, wide corridor, she glanced once more at the man beside her. In his black tuxedo and swan white dress shirt with the row of perfect, creamy white pearl studs running down the front, she thought he looked more elegant and sophisticated than any man she'd ever known. Yet there was strength in him, as well, a power in the quiet ease with which he moved and a decidedly masculine quality in his confident, self-assured walk, as though he owned the hall they walked down and with each step was declaring his right to be there.

Despite her hurt, she was fascinated by him, Sydney admitted. As angry as she'd been at his too-sudden notice of her, she couldn't deny that a tiny part of her was thrilled at the openly admiring way he had looked at her back in his suite. If only he had liked her before. If only he had liked the real Sydney, the woman she really was, before she'd been made up to look like someone else—like the beautiful blonde from the Starlight.

Just then, he caught her gaze on him and smiled, sending her heart skittering. She looked away, not wanting him to see the dismay she was sure was written across her face.

As they neared the suite where the private party was in progress, she risked another glance at him, taking in his dark, handsome features once more. The warmth of his fingers on the bare skin of her arm, holding her with almost possessive firmness, sent a warm flutter through her. No matter how angry she was with him, she couldn't deny that she was glad he was with her. Jack Ames, one immediately sensed, was a man who could—and always would—take care of himself. Going into this room full of wealthy strangers wouldn't be so hard with Jack by her side.

Outside the door, Jack stopped and turned her toward him, smiling at her.

"Before we go in, there's something I want to say, Sydney." He paused. "Back in my suite, you told me not to forget that you were the same old Syd underneath."

Surprised that he had guessed her thoughts so closely, Sydney watched him wordlessly.

"I've been thinking about that," he went on, "and I've decided it's not necessarily true. Maybe, just maybe, *this* is the real Sydney Stone."

Stunned and hurt, Sydney stared at him. Then before she could gather her thoughts, she felt his hands clasp her arms and pull her forward. He lowered his face toward hers as if to kiss her.

Sydney thrust her hands up and against his chest, shrugging out of his grasp. Furious, she yanked up the bodice of her dress.

"Just cool your jets, Jack Ames," she said, her face flushed. "Because I'm not buying it."

He stared at her with a vacant look. Then his eyes narrowed. "Buying it? What are you talking about? Buying what?"

"You know what."

"No, I don't. I don't have the faintest idea what you're talking about."

"All right." Sydney put her hands on her hips. "How come you're being so nice to me all of a sudden, huh?"

He blinked at her in confusion.

"God," she breathed, throwing her arms up in frustration. "You just don't get it, do you? Men. You're so superficial."

"What? Would you please explain what you're talking about? Why are you so angry? What did I do? Why *shouldn't* I be nice to you?"

"Because," she said hotly, then stopped. How could she explain that she wanted him to like *her*, not a fake replica of his blond girlfriend? How could she explain how important, how vitally important, that one point was? When she continued, it was in a much calmer voice. "Because you weren't so nice before. Before Claus dolled me up, you didn't like me at all."

"Didn't—" Jack sputtered. "I did, too. I liked you. I liked you a lot."

"Then what's wrong with the *old* Sydney?"

"What's wrong? Are you kidding me?"

"Oh," she said, making it a groan of disgust. "Oh, never mind. Just never mind. You'll never understand."

"Why don't you try to explain it to me?"

Yanking on the doorknob, she shook her head. "Forget it, I said. Let's just get this over with."

As she stepped across the threshold into the dimly lit foyer, she heard Jack mutter behind her, "You are the most enigmatic woman I've ever met."

"Oh, yeah? Well, at least I'm not a stuck-up snob," she whispered as a tuxedoed doorman approached them.

"Sydney, enigmatic means *mysterious*."

"Mr. Ames," the doorman said with a smile. "It's nice to see you again this evening."

Jack was frowning hard at her, his hands in his pockets.

"Mr. Ames?"

"Hmm? Oh, Walter. Hello."

"I think there's a seat for you at your usual table." Walter glanced at Sydney.

Jack straightened his shoulders and finally gave his attention to the doorman. "They've been waiting for me, have they? All right. Walter, this is Miss Stone. She'll be playing off my line of credit tonight."

Jack gave her a meaningful look. Unnecessarily, Sydney thought. He'd already gone over the rules of high-stakes gambling with her. She wouldn't see any money at all tonight, he'd told her. Everyone who could afford to be at this party took a line of credit with the casino, which they were billed for later. The only thing they played with were harmless-looking chips.

Sydney didn't know how large Jack's line was, but she gathered it was big enough. He didn't want a novice playing with thousand-dollar chips.

"Of course, Mr. Ames," Walter said, still smiling.

"Make sure she gets anything she wants."

"Of course, sir."

Taking her elbow in a tight grip, Jack steered her across the marble floor toward the double doors. From behind the glossy panels, Sydney could hear laughter and shouts of excitement.

"Just remember," Sydney said as another tuxedoed man opened the doors for them, "you've got my ten thousand dollars."

# 4

The lights and noise of the private casino dazzled Sydney. At first, she saw only a blur of colors and movement, then slowly the glitter of diamonds, the sparkle of crystal chandeliers, the brilliant plumage of evening gowns and the green baize of the gambling tables began to take shape. Yet what struck her as most nerve-racking were all the heads that turned their way and the eyes, avid with curiosity, that followed their progress into the room.

Unconsciously, she squeezed Jack's hand, and he returned the pressure soothingly.

"You're all right," he said. "Just smile, and you'll be fine."

Swallowing nervously, Sydney tried to force the corners of her mouth up. Her heart was racing, and it took all her willpower not to turn and flee the room.

"Jack! Nice to see you, buddy."

As they made their way steadily across the room, Sydney turned to try to locate the caller in the crowd.

"'Evening, Jack," a passing man in a white suit greeted.

"Mr. Ames." A waiter stepped in front of them. "Cocktail?"

"Thank you, Jay." Taking a glass of champagne from the waiter's tray, Jack handed it to Sydney. "Bring me a scotch and water. Heavy on the water."

The waiter beamed. "Yes, sir."

"Here, drink this," Jack urged her. "You look like you're going to faint."

"It's just all these people. And the lights. And the noise. Does *everybody* know you? Oh, look! Look at that woman's necklace. I don't think I've ever seen so many jewels in my life."

"Yes." Jack sighed regretfully. "It *is* a tempting sight."

"What?"

"Hey." A tall, lean man with longish blond hair pulled back in a small ponytail greeted them. "Black Jack. Long time, no see. Where've you been?"

"Quentin. How are you?"

Sydney drank down her glass of champagne and watched the two men shake hands.

"Sydney, this is an old friend of mine. Quentin Whatley. Quentin, may I introduce Sydney Stone."

Light green eyes in a tanned, appealing face smiled at her. "You may indeed. It's my pleasure, Sydney. My pleasure." He winked at Jack. "I see you've still got a few cards up your sleeve, Black Jack. Where've you been hiding this beauty? On that hellhole you call an island paradise?"

With a smooth, barely noticeable movement, Jack took Sydney's elbow in his strong fingers. "It *is* paradise. Wait until we open, Quentin. You'll be begging me for reservations."

"I'll believe it when I see it." Noticing Sydney's empty glass, Quentin stopped a waiter and exchanged it for a full one. "Are you playing poker tonight?"

"Yes. At Jamison's table."

Quentin gave a soundless whistle. "Oy-la-la. You always liked playing with the big boys. Maybe I'll come by later." He smiled at Sydney. "I could entertain Sydney while you're cheating them out of next year's tax breaks. See you, Sydney!"

Sipping the second flute of champagne, Sydney raised a hand in farewell.

"Hey, take it easy on that stuff," Jack said. "It can go right to your head."

"To tell you the truth, *Black Jack,* that doesn't sound half-bad."

Smiling, Jack shook his head and led her around a cluster of baccarat tables.

"Why did he call you that? Black Jack?"

"Because that was my game. Once upon a time, I was the best."

"Once upon a time?"

He didn't look at her. "When you're the best, it's hard to find a casino that doesn't know it."

"You mean, the casinos won't let you play blackjack anymore?"

"I believe that sums it up admirably."

At the crap table, a tall, angular woman with short black hair separated herself from the crowd and stopped Jack midstride with a touch of her fingers on his sleeve.

"Jack," she purred.

"Evana." Jack glanced at Sydney, then away. "How nice to see you."

"Not as nice as it is to see you."

"It has been a long time, and I'd love to talk, but there's a table waiting on me, so—"

"Of course." For the first time, the woman's coal black eyes flickered over Sydney, then away dismissively. "I'm staying at Caesar's this time. Give me a call."

As they moved away, Sydney mimicked, "Evana, how nice to see you."

"She's an old acquaintance."

"Old is right."

Jack grinned. "Do I detect a note of jealousy?"

Sydney scowled at him. "In your dreams, Black Jack."

In the back of the room near a wall of French doors that led onto a wide terrace, a round table covered in green baize sat a little apart from the rest of the tables. A low light illuminated the piles of chips, the stern-faced dealer and the four men studying their cards with serious expressions.

Although the men weren't playing against the casino but against one another, the Sunburst had provided a pit boss to ensure that the game was conducted honestly. The big, swarthy man was standing behind the dealer, his quick eyes catching every movement at the table.

"Is that it?" Sydney whispered.

Jack didn't have time to reply. Three of the four players rose to their feet, calling out greetings. The fourth player, a man in his mid-sixties, scowled at his cards without glancing up. From the large black cowboy hat on his head, the potbelly straining the cummerbund of his tuxedo and the fine network of thin red veins across his nose and cheeks, Sydney pinned him immediately as their man, Ryle Jamison. Behind him stood a slender, auburn-haired young woman with a flawless complexion. No older than twenty, she was wearing a tight, short white dress and long, dangling diamond earrings, one of which alone, Sydney thought ruefully, could have bought ten mobile homes of the type she lived in at Venice Beach. Sydney smiled at her.

When the introductions were over and the women seated once more on higher chairs behind the players, two hard-looking men in dark suits, who had stood discreetly in the background, came forward. With impassive faces, they handed Jack a hundred thousand dollars in chips, then retreated into the shadows once more.

As the game began, Sydney gripped the edge of her seat with her fingers and felt her mouth go dry. At first, she watched each play with breathless concentration. Each time Jack won a hand, she felt her heart soar with the keen, heady joy of victory. More often he lost, and every time the pile of chips before him shrank, Sydney's stomach tightened in knots.

By the first half hour, however, her attention had begun to wander. When Quentin Whatley suddenly appeared by her side, she smiled at him gratefully. He handed her a glass of champagne, and although she'd already drunk more than she had at Sheila's wedding, she eagerly accepted.

"How are you enjoying the game?" he asked, indicating the table.

"It's intense," she replied.

Quentin's green eyes were warm with laughter, and his gaze roved appreciatively over her face and down to her shoulders. Despite herself, Sydney enjoyed the attention. For the first time in her life, people were noticing her. She hadn't missed the envious glances of the women who strolled past and the open looks of desire from the men who hovered nearby, watching the game. Yes, she did enjoy it.

And why shouldn't she? she asked herself. She had never felt so beautiful before, and she probably never would again. Who cared if it was all a farce? Why not enjoy it while it lasted?

"Are you staying here at the Sunburst?" Quentin asked, bending closer so that he almost came between her and Jack, who was seated directly in front of her.

When she nodded, the instant disappointment on his face was obvious, and she realized he thought she was staying with Jack.

"My sister booked me a room," Sydney clarified.

She heard Jack shift restlessly in his chair.

Quentin's expression lightened. "Wonderful. So, you're on your own? Maybe we can have dinner sometime?"

Sydney glanced up at him through her eyelashes, trying a look she'd seen her sister give a hundred times. "Maybe."

"How about tonight?"

Taken back, Sydney fumbled for an answer, just as Jack rose to his feet.

"Excuse me, gentlemen," she heard him say. "Please, play the next hand without me."

Turning, he nodded at Quentin, took Sydney's arm and nearly lifted her bodily off her chair. Among the murmurs at the table, she heard him say, "Come with me."

As Jack propelled her toward the open French doors, she smiled over her shoulder at Quentin and sang out, "I'll be right back." In that quick glance, she caught a glimpse of Ryle Jamison licking his slack lips in pleasure.

"What do you think you're trying to pull?" Jack demanded when they'd reached a deserted corner of the terrace.

"Pull?" She gave him an innocent look and sipped from her champagne glass.

Impatiently, Jack snatched the glass from her fingers and set it on the railing behind him.

"You know exactly what I talking about. All right, you're gorgeous. You know it. I know it. Everybody in the place knows it. But don't go testing your new wings on my time, Sydney. You're with *me,* and in case you've forgotten, I'm trying to win five thousand for you."

"Why, Jack Ames, do I detect a note of jealousy?"

Jack's eyes narrowed dangerously. "And to think that behind those glasses lurked a first-rate femme fatale."

"A what?" Sydney watched him turn away, then called after him, "I don't even know what that is!"

With startling quickness, he turned back to her. "A she-devil. And oh, yes, you do. You know very, very well. Women like you were *born* knowing it. Like a sixth sense, you know just what buttons to push."

"That still doesn't excuse the fact that you didn't like me the way I was," Sydney blustered, vaguely aware that she felt a little drunk and a little reckless. "You weren't even remotely interested in me before you had me all spiffed up."

Jack studied her intently, his dark eyes glinting with anger. "You know what, Sydney? You couldn't be more wrong about that. I liked you much better before."

Speechless, Sydney watched him stride through the French doors as a slow, hot flush crept up her cheeks.

On his way back to the table, Jack noticed his shoulders were tense with anger and his face stiff from frowning. With an effort, he softened his expression, even managed to smile at several of the players as he took his seat. Yet inside, he was simmering.

He'd reached the most demanding part of the plan, the point at which his timing and responses were crucial. He had to have a clear head, yet his thinking was anything but level at the moment.

Damn her, he cursed silently, picking up a card and scrutinizing it with forced nonchalance. Unexpectedly, ridiculously, he was letting Sydney Stone and her childishly blatant flirting get to him, and he wasn't sure how or why or even when she'd managed *that* feat. It had been a long time since anyone had roused his emotions the way she did. Moreover, her timing couldn't have been worse if she'd tried.

Stirring restlessly in his seat, he stared determinedly at his cards. He *would* concentrate, he ordered himself sternly. He had a job to do. A difficult, delicate plan to pull off. Unless he wanted to lose every cent he'd wagered—most of his capital and Sydney's, too—he would need all his wits about him.

Yet, he again raised his eyes from his cards, unaware he was gazing at the doors to the terrace with a distracted expression until the dealer called his name a third time.

For a long while, Sydney stood alone on the terrace. The night sky was clear and studded with thousands of tiny stars. A warm, balmy breeze blew across the desert valley to lift the curling wisps of newly highlighted hair around her face. Beyond the French doors, she could hear the sounds of laughter and the din of excited voices.

Miserably, she leaned against the railing and gazed at the sky. She hated to admit it, but there was some truth to what Jack had said. Oh, she was still angry. Although, if she was honest, *hurt* might be the better word. She still thought that people ought to like one another because of who they were inside, not how they looked.

Yet Jack had a point. Tonight, who she was inside probably wasn't anything to brag about. She'd been surly and ungrateful. She'd flirted, even when she knew it might distract Jack from the game. It wasn't Jack's fault, she finally concluded, that she didn't feel like the glamorous, self-confident image she was presenting this evening.

For a few more moments, Sydney stood beside the railing, thinking about the black-haired man playing poker at the table inside. The sudden ache in her chest made her close her eyes. If she'd ever dreamed about the perfect man, she knew Jack Ames would fit it to a tee. Not only was he devastatingly handsome, elegantly sophisticated and exotically intriguing, he was also gallant.

Maybe he hadn't looked twice at her before—not as a woman, anyhow. But he had told Claus about meeting her. He'd even called her interesting. And when it came right down to it, he'd agreed to help her out—her, a perfect stranger.

Sydney sighed deeply. It was just too bad she couldn't have met him in another life.

When she stepped through the French doors, her glance caught Jack's immediately. Stony-faced, he gazed at her from under the circle of light around the table. Smoothing the sides of her dress with her palms, she nodded at him, then gave him a small, tentative smile.

His brilliantly answering smile of relief was all the invitation she needed. As she scooted onto her chair behind him, Sydney leaned forward.

"Did I miss anything?" she whispered beside his ear.

His dark eyes sparkled as he smiled at her over his shoulder. "No, Sydney. You haven't missed a thing. And I'm beginning to think you never do." More softly, he added, "Welcome back."

She peered around the table. "Did, um, Quentin leave?"

"Yes, he suddenly remembered he had a pressing engagement elsewhere." Jack started to turn back to the table, then paused. "It's not any of my business you who associate with, Sydney, but perhaps I should have told you that his real name is Douglas Whatley. Quentin is just a nickname.''

"Oh?"

"Someone once called him by the name of a certain institution he has unfortunately visited a number of times. Perhaps you've heard of it? San Quentin? For regrettable reasons, the name has stuck.''

"Oh.'' Sydney gave a mock grimace. "You sure have some interesting friends, Jack Ames.''

His smile widened. "Don't I, though?''

"Mr. Ames,'' the dealer called politely. "It's your bet.''

With a final smile for her, Jack fanned out his cards, and Sydney caught a glimpse of three queens. Quickly, she hid her smile as Jack asked for two cards. Yet when the hand was over and the men laid their cards on the table, she saw that, in Jack's five cards, there was now only one queen. As he composedly watched the dealer scoop up his precious chips and arrange them before Ryle Jamison, Sydney stared at the back of Jack's head.

What in the world was he thinking of, she silently fumed. He'd given up two of his three queens, a certain winning hand.

Her gaze fell on Jamison, who was gloating over his growing stacks of chips. And suddenly she understood. Jack was letting the man win. He was fattening him up before the kill.

Silently, Sydney watched the game with renewed confidence, although she was unable to see Jack's cards again without leaning over him in an obvious way. However, when Jack lost three hands in a row, she began to wonder if he really knew what he was doing.

As hand after hand was dealt, Sydney sat in trepidation and frustration. With distaste sour in her mouth, she watched Ryle Jamison across the table. Again and again, the fat man turned to smack the lovely young woman behind him on the rear end, and Sydney began to feel real sympathy for her.

Nearly two hours into the game, the guards came forward again, distributing chips to three of the men around the table. Jack accepted another hundred and fifty thousand dollars' worth of chips and added them to the depleted stacks already in front of him.

Finally unable to help herself, Sydney reached forward and touched his shoulder. Beneath the rich, black cloth of his tuxedo, his muscles were as hard as steel. But when he swiveled to look at her, his smile was light and easy. In that moment, she understood what a gambler, a *real* gambler, was—a man who showed no fear.

Jamison's quick, ferretlike eyes took in the glance that passed between them and Jack's new supply of chips.

Jamison grunted and shifted in his seat. "Scratch my back, honey," he said to the young woman, who obeyed without altering her vacant expression. "No, no. Not there. Over to the right. Lower. Lower! Yeah. Right there. Good. All right. All right, I said. That's enough, damn you."

Two of the men at the table kept their heads down, studiously examining their cards, as if trying to hide their dislike. Jack stared straight at Jamison.

"Your call," Jack said.

"Yeah. Yeah. I know what I'm doing," the Texan drawled meanly. "Can't say the same about you, though, can we... Black Jack?" He drew out the nickname with a sneer.

Jack sat still and calm. Sydney squirmed angrily.

"Heard you've been having a little trouble with that hotel of yours." Jamison wet his lips. "Not surprising, I guess."

"It's a resort," Jack said, his voice low. "And everything is just fine with our renovations."

"Our? Thought Tynsdale pulled out on you. Isn't that what you heard, Moynihan?"

Moynihan dipped his head, pretending to study his cards.

"When big financial backing like that pulls out, it spells trouble to me." Jamison smiled slyly at Jack. "'Course, everyone knows things haven't been going well for you since that terrible accident."

Furious at the man's taunting, Sydney had to bite her lip to keep from saying something nasty.

Jack's head snapped up, and he stared at Jamison for a long moment. "What's that supposed to mean?" He held his cards carelessly, and the strain in his voice made Sydney flinch.

Jamison's eyes glittered behind his stacks of chips. "'Course, you weren't anywhere around there when it happened. So you don't know much about it, do you?" He gave a snigger, as though only a complete idiot would believe such a story.

"I *wasn't* there," Jack insisted.

Anxiously, Sydney concentrated on the back of Jack's head, willing him to calm down.

"It's your bet, Mr. Everett," the dealer said quietly but firmly in an attempt to get the game back under control.

But the player named Everett was staring in fascination at Jamison, then back to Jack.

"Of course you weren't. You weren't anywhere near there." Jamison turned to the girl behind him and gave her a swat of amusement, as though including her in the joke. The girl gazed ahead blankly.

"What exactly are you implying?"

The sharp edge in Jack's voice alarmed Sydney. Was he finally cracking? Had he pushed his luck too far this time?

"Nothing, Ames. I ain't saying nothing. Except that maybe that little accident did something to your nerves. If it *was* an accident. You sure haven't been playing very well, has he, boys?" Suddenly, Jamison's beady eyes fixed on Sydney. "Can't even seem to control your women anymore."

Before she knew what she was doing, Sydney was on her feet. "Oh, and I suppose slapping young girls around in public is your idea of foreplay, you fat, old pervert."

Jamison grinned at her, looking delighted with her outburst.

"Sydney, sit down," Jack murmured.

"I will not. He's disgusting. How can you let him talk to—"

"Shut up," Jack barked, keeping his back to her.

Breathing hard, Sydney glared at the men around the table. The young woman behind Jamison averted her eyes. With great reluctance, Sydney finally sat down.

"Gentlemen," the dealer said softly, "if you'll place your bets now."

For a few, short minutes, the game continued. With real apprehension now, Sydney saw Jack light a cigarette with hands that trembled ever so slightly. He kept a constant, furious stare on Jamison.

"And I'll raise—" Jamison stared back at Jack "—another thirty thousand dollars."

Everett laid his cards facedown with a sigh. The other two players looked surprised but interested.

"Pete," Jack called gruffly to the pit boss. "Get over here."

Sydney felt her heart skip a beat.

"Mr. Ames?" the man asked.

"I want another two hundred and fifty thousand dollars."

"Sir?"

Sydney put her hand on Jack's shoulder. "Jack—" She stopped as he shrugged her hand away.

"I *said* another two hundred and fifty thousand dollars," Jack ordered from between his teeth.

"Yes, sir."

When the chips were laid before him, Jack spread his hands and pushed the whole pile forward. Coldly, he glared at Jamison.

"I'll see you, and raise you another two hundred and eighty-three thousand."

"Oh, God," Sydney whispered quietly as the blood drained from her face. He *had* cracked. Jack was putting all his money—*her* money, too—on one hand. What had she been thinking when she asked him to gamble with her sister's money?

"Jack," she said, her voice taut with anxiety.

He ignored her.

Jamison was smiling, his little eyes gleaming. "And I'll see you," he said slowly. "Though not, I'm afraid, in the winner's circle."

"I can't stand this," Sydney moaned. "I can't watch this, Jack."

Jamison's smile widened at her words. When Jack didn't bother to glance back at her, she slipped off her chair. Reaching out, she nearly touched his shoulder, then merely turned away and crept into the crowd that had begun to gather around the table.

Blindly, Sydney made her way to the ladies' room and stumbled in. Leaning on the counter, she gazed at her own reflection. Her eyes were dark with worry and her skin was pale.

My God, she thought in a sudden panic. What would she say to Sheila? She'd been so certain that Jack would win the five thousand dollars for them. Now she was going to have to tell her sister she'd lost even their initial ten thousand! How could she do that? How could she have done this to Sheila?

"Excuse me," Sydney heard from behind her. Raising her eyes, she met the smile of the young woman who had stood behind Jamison. Her animated expression was so unlike the blank look of boredom she'd worn all evening that Sydney could only stare.

"I just wanted to thank you," the woman said. "For telling Ryle off. I've wanted to say something like that to him all night, but I didn't have the nerve."

Sydney blinked at her.

"So, well, just thank you."

Sydney watched through the mirror as Jamison's girl-friend put a hand on the door. "Are you going back to the table?" she suddenly asked.

Pausing, the woman smiled and shook her head. "No, not now. I think I'm just going to go home."

When Sydney finally decided she could no longer avoid it and opened the rest-room door, she saw Jack hovering nearby. Instantly, her worst fears were confirmed. He wouldn't meet her eyes.

In silence, they walked through the double doors and into the foyer. When he took her elbow gently in his hand, Sydney thought she might burst into tears.

"Your timing, Sydney," Jack said quietly as they stepped into the hall outside, "was impeccable."

Sydney squeezed her eyes tightly shut. "I'm sorry. I just couldn't sit there any longer."

"No, Sydney. I meant that you were wonderful."

The doors closed behind them, and in the empty corridor, Jack suddenly scooped her up in a bear hug and swung her around.

"You were brilliant. Fantastic. My God, what a team." He danced with her down the hall, her legs dangling above the floor. "One big hand, Sydney. I wanted to get that loudmouthed buffoon with just one big hand. And you helped me draw him in. Hell, you were sensational."

"I was?"

"He thought he could shake me. He thought he might be roping me in, and your little outburst clinched it for him. You convinced him, and he dived in headfirst. Then," Jack went on gleefully, "then—oh, and what a touch, Sydney—then you got up from the table. You were brilliant. He thought he had me for certain."

Jack's nose was two inches from her's, and Sydney stared into his laughing black eyes.

"Do you mean we *won?*"

"Won? With three aces and a jack? We cleaned up. We picked Jamison up and shook his pockets empty. Oh, yes, we won...about seven hundred and twenty-three thousand dollars, Sydney."

"*What?*"

"It's lobster and champagne for us tonight."

"How much did you say?" she cried in excitement. "How much did we win?"

Stopping in the center of the corridor, he repeated, "Seven hundred and twenty-three thousand dollars. Give or take a few thousand. I figure, you just made yourself fifteen thousand above your initial investment. Not bad for a night's work, hmm?"

"I can't believe it," Sydney breathed in astonishment, and then she was laughing, her eyes shining into his.

She felt the stillness in his body first as he held her up and against him. Then a change came over his face. Slowly, his grin faded and was replaced by a quiet, somber intensity. Gently, he lowered her to her feet but didn't release her.

"You know, I'm beginning to suspect that I might just have found Lady Luck," he said softly. His hand moved up from her arm and slid across her bare shoulder to come to rest in her hair. "Actually, I think I've done more than just found her."

Sydney's heart skittered, and she raised her hands to his chest, pressing her palms flat against the cool smoothness of his tuxedo. She could feel the heat of his body through the soft fabric.

"Jack—" She faltered.

"In fact, I think I could fall for her," he went on, weaving his fingers through her curls.

She tried to step back and out of his encircling arms, but somehow she just couldn't make herself. She felt mesmerized by the black depths of his eyes and dazed by the sudden closeness of his body. His hand was strong yet gentle against the bare skin of her back, pressing her closer to him, while his other hand tilted back her face.

"Jack," she protested weakly again.

"I don't know, though," he murmured, his mouth moving closer to hers. "Lady Luck is notoriously fickle. Should I take my chances, Sydney?"

He continued to pull her firmly against him, and when her breasts touched his chest, her breath caught in her throat.

"Oh, Jack," she said laughingly, trying to lighten the mood as she pushed against him. "You don't need luck. You're smart enough without—"

"Oh, but I do," he said, tightening his arms around her. "Every man needs luck, Sydney."

At the first touch of his lips against hers, Sydney felt her knees weaken. Soft and beguiling, his lips barely brushed hers, as though he was testing the waters. She tried to calm her racing heart, tried to fight the tingling rush that overcame her at his touch, but when his kiss grew bolder and more possessive, she felt her hands clutch at his lapels.

Long and hard, his mouth covered hers, his lips persuading, coaxing, teasing until she felt herself kiss him back. With a sigh of pleasure, he gathered her more closely, holding her against the hard, lean length of his body.

Dreamlike, she felt her body respond as his lips grew more demanding. Helplessly, she felt herself being swept away by the new and heady intimacy of his lips on hers and her body against his.

When he finally raised his head, stepping back from her, she could only gaze dumbly up at him. Dazed and confused, she saw him smile at her.

"Consider that a promise, Lady Luck," he said thickly. "An open invitation."

In wonder, Sydney raised a finger to her tingling lips, and he gave a low chuckle.

"But first, I think I owe you dinner." With a hand on the small of her back, he led her down the corridor, his hand slipping a little lower as they reached the elevator, then a little lower still as they entered the car.

Sydney's eyes widened in shock.

"By the way, Sydney," he said, punching the button for the tenth floor. "You have one hell of a great walk."

She stared, still stupefied. "I do?"

"Yes, you do. Like a corkscrew. All circular curves and smooth twists. Drives me crazy."

The elevator doors opened, and he helped her out. "So what'll it be? We're celebrating tonight. Should we have champagne and lobster? Oysters Rockefeller? Caviar?"

"Yes," she said in a stunned voice.

"Yes?" Jack halted outside the door, then laughed. "Claus already loves you. Now he'll worship you for sure."

# 5

After splashing cool water on her flushed face in the enormous, marble-tiled bathroom, kicking off her high heels and curling onto a sofa in the living room of Jack's suite, Sydney felt she once more had herself in hand. She refused Jack's offer of champagne, sensing that she would need all her wits about her if she was going to get through the rest of the evening without making a fool of herself. Sipping a diet soda, she watched him settle on the floor at her feet.

From the kitchen, she could hear the clanking of pots and the whir of a blender as Claus happily busied himself preparing their late-night celebration.

"Here's to a winning team," Jack said, raising his champagne flute and clinking it against her soda glass. "What are you going to do with your share of the money we won?"

Sydney shrugged. "Pay off the blackmailer."

"Yes, I know that. I meant the rest of it. There'll be enough left for you to buy something special, I think. What have you always dreamed of having?"

Silently, she stirred the ice in her glass with a finger, concentrating on the swirling cubes as though they were the most fascinating thing she'd ever seen. If the fifteen thousand extra was hers, she knew exactly what she'd do with it. She'd pay off her telephone bill, buy her mother a new dishwasher and take some time off from the restaurant to concentrate on her photography. It was a tempting thought.

But then, of course, the money wasn't really hers, and as much as she loved her sister, she had to admit that Sheila wasn't the type to share her winnings with anyone else.

"I don't know," she lied quietly. "I'll think of something."

Jack leaned back against the sofa, his face close to her legs. "I bet you will. We did a good night's work. You and me, Sydney. Lord, what I wouldn't have given to have known you in the old days."

His words reminded her of Jamison's taunts, which had mystified her at the time. A lot of things puzzled her about Jack, she was discovering. "The old days?" she asked.

Jack smiled and lifted his glass to his lips. "The *very* old days. A million years ago."

Sydney studied him. "Jack, what did Jamison mean about an accident? The way you reacted, I thought you were really mad."

"Mad? No." He shook his head. "I wanted him to think I was. That's all. It was part of the game. No, I wasn't angry. After all, I know what really happened."

Sydney set her glass on the table beside her. "What do you mean? What really happened?"

He glanced at her hesitantly. Reaching across the table, he flipped open a cigarette box, took one and lit it. "A few years ago, I was in a different sort of, well, business." He paused, seeming to gauge her reaction. "It was very lucrative."

"You mean, illegal."

"I didn't say that. But, yes. It was." He paused again, blowing out smoke in a long, slow stream. "I made a lot of money in the casinos at Monte Carlo and places like that, not always in a strictly honest way. And I made a lot more by relieving very wealthy people of their jewels."

Sydney ran the tip of her tongue over her bottom lip. Her mouth felt dry. "You were a con man and a thief," she said flatly.

He didn't reply.

"I never met anyone like that before," she said a bit nervously.

When he still didn't speak, but only watched her guardedly, she asked, "You aren't now, though. Are you?" Her voice sounded strained. "I mean, you aren't those things now, are you?"

He smiled at her. "No, Sydney, I'm not. Not at all. I quit awhile ago. Now I'm just a very ordinary, very reputable resort owner. A little poorer maybe. Still, I own a nice piece of land on a small island in the Bahamas called San Miguel, and I've been renovating the old governor's mansion. It's cost quite a bundle, but I think when I'm done, it will be worth it."

"What made you quit?"

Unexpectedly, his smile dimmed, and he turned his eyes away.

"I'm sorry," she began. "It's none of my business what—"

"It's all right." Tamping down his cigarette, Jack finished his champagne and lifted the bottle from the silver ice bucket. She watched him pour himself another glass.

"I used to work off and on with a partner. An old friend of mine named Frenchie. Actually, a relation. He married my cousin." Jack sipped from his glass. "We were on a job in the Riviera. The kind of thing we'd done a dozen times before. Off the roof and onto a balcony in the middle of the night, back onto the roof and across to the next building...and away. It was very clean and quick. No one ever knew we were there. Until they opened their jewel cases, of course."

Spellbound, Sydney hugged her knees, listening raptly.

"I don't know what happened. Believe me, I've asked myself a thousand times. We'd already been in and had the jewels on us. One of the pieces was a diamond and sapphire tiara, I remember. Lovely. I'd already made it to the ground without any problems. It wasn't even a difficult climb, once you got past the first balcony. But something happened. Something went wrong."

Jack looked across the room, his gaze remote, as though reliving that night all over again. The expression on his face was one of undisguised anguish. "Frenchie was older than I was. Although he refused to admit it, I knew for a while that he was getting too old for that kind of work."

"What happened?" Sydney asked softly.

"I don't know. He just didn't make it. Maybe he slipped. Maybe he lost his nerve. Maybe something startled him. No one will ever know. He fell four stories. I believe he died instantly."

"Oh, God." Sydney moved to touch his shoulder, but something in his voice stopped her.

"Do you know what the worst part was? I mean later, when I had time to think about it. The worst thing was that I didn't stay with him . . . with his . . . with the body." There was a jagged edge in his voice. "I wanted to. I wanted to stay there with him. I couldn't bear to leave him crushed and broken. I couldn't stand to think of him lying there like that until someone discovered him. But if I'd stayed, it would have meant certain arrest. So I left him."

Sydney's throat tightened. "I'm sorry."

He glanced up at her with shadowed eyes, then gave her a small smile. "So am I. I miss him a great deal sometimes."

"It's not your fault, you know. It's not your fault you couldn't stay with him."

"Of course not," he said, but his words were bitter. "It's never anyone's fault."

"Jack—"

"So that's when I got out. I suppose you could say it was the excuse I was looking for. No one ever got hurt by anything we did, but still—I'd planned to retire soon to San Miguel, anyway."

"Are you glad you did? Retire, I mean."

The sadness coloring his smile disappeared. "I'm very glad. I wouldn't have met you if I hadn't, would I?"

Sydney studied her glass of soda on the table.

"So, what's *your* story, Sydney Stone?" he asked as though sensing her discomfort. "Tell me about yourself."

With a small laugh, she shook her head. "There's nothing to tell. You already know everything about me."

"Now, that's not true. Where are you from? Tell me about your family. I want to know everything about you."

She grimaced. "All right. Well, my parents still live in Pasadena. Dad's in waste removal." She shot him a quick, bright smile. "You aren't supposed to call them garbagemen anymore. And I have an older sister, Sheila."

"Sheila and Sydney Stone?" he asked playfully.

She grinned. "I guess my parents were into that consonant thing. Allit-something."

"Alliteration?"

"Yeah. Actually, Sheila is Sheila Crane now. She married Ambrose Crane a few years ago."

"Ambrose Crane? The name sounds familiar."

"He's a bigwig in Connecticut politics."

Jack nodded. "That's right. Attorney general or something. Isn't he running for the senate?"

Sydney nodded. "Yeah. Which thrills my sister. And my parents."

"But not you?"

"Well, let's just say *I* wouldn't vote for him. Although, thank goodness, living in California, I don't have to worry about it."

Jack chuckled. "Typical politician, hmm?"

"Worse." She giggled with him. "I don't know how he does it, but he could sell snow to Eskimos."

"Ah," Jack teased. "A con man."

"Exactly."

Jack's smile didn't waver, but she could see a speculative look cross his face, a short hesitation that told her he was uncertain about what he wanted to say.

"If you don't mind my asking," he finally said, sipping his champagne with pretended nonchalance, "how did you get involved with this guy? The one who's blackmailing you?"

Sydney's own smile faded. She looked away, unwilling to let him see her eyes for fear he might read the lie there.

"Oh, it was a long time ago," she said, her voice as purposefully airy as his.

"Hmm." He swirled the champagne, not drinking. "So, what's his name?"

She shot him a look of alarm. "I don't know," she said truthfully. "He's not the one who...well, took the pictures. I'm not even sure how he got a hold of them."

"Hmm," Jack repeated thoughtfully.

Something threatening, almost dangerously protective, in his manner sent off warning bells in her head.

"Look, Jack," she told him, "this is my problem. Don't start getting any macho ideas about interfering."

"But if I can help—"

"No," Sydney said sternly, cutting him off. "I'm a big girl, and I'm used to taking care of myself. I can handle this—"

From the direction of the kitchen came a discreet cough. With a swell of relief, Sydney turned, eager to drop the subject of her sister's troubles—and her own falsehoods. Claus lumbered toward them with a laden tray, looking pleased as punch.

"Lobster Newburg. Beluga caviar. Oysters Rockefeller. And because it's a special occasion, saveloy with truffles in brioche." Setting down the heavy tray as easily as if it were a teacup, he stood back and beamed at them. "Enjoy."

Sydney gaped at the feast. "Claus, you're a miracle worker."

"Where are you going?" Jack called as the big man backed away. "Stay and celebrate with us."

"No, thanks. I want to catch the end of Letterman."

"Claus loves David Letterman," Jack explained to Sydney. "Ever since he had Julia Child on his program."

"The guy's got class," Claus declared, making Sydney laugh.

Helping themselves to oysters, dipping small crunchy crackers into salty caviar and making appreciative noises as they forked up bites of succulent lobster, Jack and Sydney smiled at each other. Claus had brought out a fresh bottle of champagne, and Jack uncorked it. Sydney squealed at the loud bang and the small jet of foam that shot from the bottle.

Suddenly happy again, she leaned back against the peach-colored cushions, licking caviar from her fingertips and wondering what the other waitresses at Vernon's would say if they could see her now. With her new hairstyle and clothes, she guessed they wouldn't even recognize her.

Certainly, if they could see the warm, intense way Jack was looking at her, they would have been astonished. Come to think of it, she was astonished. What was more, she was almost beginning to be fooled herself.

"...of course, the deluxe cabanas," he was saying, "have the best view of the bay and the ocean. A minute's walk from the beach. Everything your heart desires, and only a phone call away. That's the principal idea behind the resort. It will be a place where even those used to being pampered will feel spoiled."

Only half listening to him, Sydney nibbled a strawberry and wondered what trick of fate had given her this one night of magic. Because it *was* a trick. The whole evening, everything she was pretending to be, was an illusion. She couldn't afford to forget that, she told herself. It was only one night. Tomorrow morning, she was going to wake up and face a lifetime of being plain old Syd Stone again.

"...and the bougainvillea is in bloom year-round." Jack paused, studied her and frowned. "I've been going on and on, haven't I? Sorry about that. Comes from being obsessed by a project."

"I think your resort sounds beautiful," Sydney said politely. She swung her legs off the couch. "Maybe someday I'll win the lottery or something and come stay there."

"Sydney," Jack began, his voice low and full of meaning.

"I'd better go now." With an attempt at breeziness, she tossed her napkin on the table and sat up. "Thanks for...well, for everything. For the money. The dinner." She swallowed and tried to smile. "I'll never forget this night."

Before she could stand, Jack reached for her hand.

"It doesn't have to be over."

Sydney felt her heartbeat trip, then she looked away and eased her hand from his. "Yes, it does."

Pulling himself to his feet, Jack stood beside the sofa, gazing down at her. "Stay with me, Sydney," he said softly. "Stay the night."

Wordlessly, Sydney shook her head.

Jack lowered himself to the sofa to sit beside her, watching her intently. "You've enjoyed tonight. I know you have. And I don't think you want it to end any more than I do."

Closing her eyes, Sydney fought the strange new longing she'd felt growing in her ever since she'd first seen Jack in the Starlight. Yet try as she might to deny it, she knew he was right.

She did enjoy being with him. She didn't want the night to end. But what she wanted didn't matter. Sooner or later, the night would be over and she'd be back pouring grainy coffee, serving thin burgers and sweeping up sand from the greasy floor of Vernon's shabby beachside restaurant.

That was her life and her future. As long as she didn't let her imagination run away with her, she could accept the concept just fine. But the longer she played at this glamorous game of pretend, the harder it was going to be to accept the inevitable reality.

Slowly, hesitantly, she tried to explain. "This isn't me, Jack. This isn't my world. This isn't what I really look like or who I really am. You know that. I was just pretending for tonight. But the real Syd Stone... Well, you don't know me.''

"I think I do. I don't think I could have helped it. Sydney, you are one of the most forthright, honest people I've ever met. There's not a deceptive bone in your body. And I hate to break this to you, but you're not really that good an actress. I think I do know you.''

Sydney shook her head. "No. No, you don't," she said vehemently.

Jack studied her for a moment. At last, he said, "All right. Then tell me. Who's Sydney Stone? Who is she really?''

Sydney stared down at the carpet, and a dozen answers flashed through her mind. Who was she? She was the fat, lonely girl who had tried so hard to be helpful her whole life and who had grown used to being overlooked. She was the woman who couldn't forget the humiliation or the pain of her youth. She was the hardworking waitress who had found a way to live with her disappointments and who didn't want to threaten the self-made—the *only*—security she'd ever known.

Yes, maybe her life was boring and uneventful. But it was her life. It was who she was. And the thought of trying to be something more was terrifying.

"I'm nobody. Nobody special," she finally murmured so softly he had to bend closer to hear. "And I *like* it that way."

Jack's face registered surprise and dismay. Heavily, he leaned back against the sofa cushions and stared at her.

"My God, Sydney. What ever happened to make you so afraid? So afraid of life?''

At his words, her head snapped up, and she gave him a quick, hot look. "I'm not afraid.''

"Oh, yes, you are. You've convinced yourself that you're a plain 'nobody' because it's comfortable. Because it's safe. But you're not a coward, Sydney. That I *do* know. So it must be eating you up inside having to—''

Sydney jumped to her feet. "I don't have to listen to this."

Jack rose also. "No, you don't have to listen to me. But you should."

"Why should I? So you can look down your perfect, rich, snooty nose at me?"

Jack's eyes widened in surprise, then his mouth hardened. "That's the second time tonight you've called me a snob. I'd like to know what I could have possibly done to give you that impression. Frankly, I resent it. I am *not* a—"

"You didn't look twice at me when I wasn't made up to fit your idea of glamorous."

Exhaling rapidly, he glanced at the ceiling in frustration. "Oh, I see. We're back to that."

"Yes, we're back to that," Sydney mimicked angrily, but she knew she was only blustering. More weakly, she added, "Please, I don't want to fight. I had a great time tonight. I really did. And I'm very grateful for everything you've done."

"Gratitude," Jack muttered grudgingly, "was not the emotion I was hoping for."

Suddenly, a small smile touched her lips. "How about, I'm really glad I met you?"

"That's a little better."

Sydney's smile was soft. "So, couldn't we say goodbye as friends?"

Jack's expression froze. "Goodbye? I thought you were staying until you heard from the blackm—"

"All right, then. Good night?"

Jack couldn't remember the last time he'd felt so keyed up and restless. Not even in the old days after he'd pulled a job, when his nerves felt raw and adrenaline kept him awake until dawn, had he felt this agitated. Probably because, no matter how dangerous the job, he'd always known that he was in perfect control. He couldn't say that now.

Sydney Stone, unlike any other woman he'd ever known, was completely unreadable. Just when he thought everything was fine, she did something unexpected, leaving him stymied and frustrated. Enigmatic, he'd called her tonight, hadn't he? Well, enigmatic was damned right.

When she'd gathered together her purse and clothes from the guest room in his suite and gravely accepted twenty thousand dollars in cash from him, she'd finally gone, leaving him with a feeling of emptiness and anticlimax. The huge suite seemed suddenly too quiet, like a deserted theater after the curtain has fallen, the lights have been doused and the audience has gone home.

Aimlessly, Jack wandered through the silent living room, glancing at the table with the remains of their celebratory dinner and scowling. Dropping to a chair, he lit a cigarette absently, letting it burn unheeded between his fingers.

Sydney Stone, he decided thoughtfully, was the most intriguing, irritating woman he'd ever met. The way she'd laughed when he told her they'd won and the way she'd looked at him with those wide blue eyes when she'd said goodbye were not images a man could easily forget.

Yet he was certain that forget was exactly what she wanted him to do. It was clear that, whatever fragile bond had begun to grow between them tonight, she'd been determined to get free of it. A small part of him knew that the wisest thing to do was to accept her retreat with good grace. Go about his business and forget Sydney Stone and her problems.

But he knew he wouldn't listen to that advice. Something about her had touched him in a way he had never been affected before. Her quick intelligence and unpretentious honesty captivated him. She was beautiful, spontaneous and daring, and yet she wouldn't, or couldn't, see that. My God, he wondered, what kind of a life had she endured to hold such a low opinion of herself?

It wasn't going to be easy. He already knew she was stubborn. But then, he wasn't the sort of man who was daunted at the first show of resistance. No, he wasn't going to let Sydney walk away that easily.

Because somehow, he suspected, it was now or never. Women like her didn't come along every day, and a wise man took his chances where he found them. If she was reluctant, if she needed some convincing, well, he'd played against tougher odds. In fact, that was the part of his reputation he valued most—when he gambled, even on a long shot, everyone knew he played to win.

And so far, he usually had.

Sydney wasn't sure whether she felt more like weeping or laughing as she shuffled down the hall to her room, lugging her bulging purse behind her. Crammed with her old clothes and the precious cash that meant Sheila's release from the blackmailer's clutches, the purse was awkward to carry, but she kept a deathlike grip on it until she reached the door of her hotel room and fumbled for the key.

If only he hadn't been so nice at the end, Sydney wanted to wail, searching through the disordered depths of the purse. She knew she'd have been a fool to stay with Jack. There was never any question of her doing that. But Jack's disappointment had only made it more difficult to do the right thing.

Finally producing the key, Sydney bent forward. As she reached out to slip it in the lock, the slight touch of her hand sent the door swinging slowly, ominously, open. Instantly she froze, her heart in her throat.

For a long, terrified moment she could do nothing but stand in the doorway, rooted to the spot. The hair on the back of her neck prickled, and she stared ahead with wide, frightened eyes.

The room was empty. That fact slowly came home to her. There was nowhere for anyone to hide in the small, economy-size hotel room. But they'd made sure she would know they'd been there.

Gradually, Sydney felt the blood return to her face, and the eerie tingling of her skin began to fade. As though she'd been smothering, she suddenly took a deep, gulping breath and inched forward a few steps.

It looked as though a tornado had swept through her room, flinging all the clothes from her closet, ripping the bedspread and sheets from the bed and emptying the drawers of the small dresser onto the floor. With a muffled cry, she saw her one good suitcase had been destroyed, slashed to ribbons and ripped apart. Dismayed, she turned around slowly, staring in disbelief at the chaos and destruction.

There was something malicious and cruel about the damage. The complete and utter savagery of the vandalism was terrifying. Stunned and frightened, Sydney numbly picked her way back across the littered floor toward the door, then suddenly turned and fled down the corridor.

Jack answered the loud, repeated knocks clad only in his pajama bottoms. The moment he saw Sydney's face, he dropped the newspaper he'd been reading. Gripping the top of her arms, he pulled her into the suite, his heart stilled by the fear and panic in her blue eyes.

"My God," he exclaimed. "What's happened?"

She was shivering, her teeth chattering audibly, and her face was alarmingly white. Clutching her enormous purse against her, she cried, "They destroyed everything. They didn't just take things, they destroyed everything."

With a black look, Jack demanded, "Who did? Who did what, Sydney?"

"My room," she cried a little wildly. "Someone robbed me. But they didn't just rob me. Oh, Jack. They went through and destroyed everything in the room."

"What?"

"It's horrible. Really evil. Oh, God. I can't believe this. I can't. Why would someone do something so...so mean?"

Jack's expression grew more dangerous. "Someone vandalized your room?"

She nodded, still shivering, and he realized she was about to go limp in his grasp. Quickly, he half walked, half carried her to the nearest chair and plunked her firmly down in it.

"Take a deep breath, Sydney," he said, rubbing her hands. "It's going to be okay. You're safe now."

Frightened blue eyes gazed up at him. "Someone was in there. In my room. Ripping apart all my things. Taking my—"

Suddenly, she gasped, a hand flying up to cover her mouth. "My camera. Oh, no. My camera," she wailed and looked as though she was about to cry. "It took me two and a half years to save for that camera. Oh, I can't believe this!"

"Look," Jack said sternly, kneeling in front of her, "you've got to calm down. We'll take care of this, but you have to get hold of yourself."

"But my camera—"

"I'll take care of it. Here, lean back." Unceremoniously shoving her back into the chair, he rose, strode to the liquor cabinet and pulled out a bottle of brandy. "You've had a fright, and you're white as a sheet. Take a sip of this," he ordered, thrusting the bottle at her.

Even her lips were pale as she put the bottle to them, drank and sputtered. "Oh, my God. That's worse than fainting," she gasped, coughing. "That stuff's awful. Uck. What is it?"

"Forty-year-old brandy." Taking it from her, he glanced at the bottle, shrugged and took a long swig, himself. "All right, tell me again—slowly this time—what happened."

"I went down to my room and was about to put the key in the lock." She shook her head as he offered her the bottle of brandy, then reluctantly accepted it and took another small sip. "The door was already open, though," she continued, her voice stronger. "It was really spooky. It just sort of opened by itself. Then I saw the room."

"There wasn't anybody—"

"Oh, no." Once more, she took the bottle from him and drank. "No one. Are you kidding? I wouldn't have gone in if someone was still there."

"You went in?" Jack gave her a look of alarm and reached for the bottle to take another drink himself. "How could you do that? They might have been hiding in there. Lying in wait for you."

Sydney shook her head, then gave a faint smile. "No way. My whole room's about the size of one of your closets. No one was there. I'm sure of it."

"Still..."

She took the bottle from him and raised it. "You know, this stuff isn't that bad. Once you get used to it."

"Listen," Jack said. "You sit here. Don't move. And don't finish off that bottle or you'll really feel ill. I'm going down to your room."

Sydney stared at him. "You're *what?*"

"I'm going down there. Then I'm calling hotel security."

"Oh, Jack. Don't go. What if they come back?"

The smile that crossed his face was not completely pleasant. "That would be a bit of luck, wouldn't it?"

## 6

By the time Jack returned to his suite, he was silent and disturbed. Sydney was still where he'd left her, sitting on the edge of the chair with the brandy bottle at her feet and her eyes on the door. He paused briefly, then shut the door and set her camera case on the table beside it.

"My camera!" she cried, delighted. "Oh, thank heavens, they didn't take my camera."

Silently, Jack studied her, his arms folded across his silk bathrobe.

"Thanks, Jack."

He considered her thoughtfully. What had she said to him earlier? That he didn't know her? Maybe there was more to that statement than he'd originally believed. After all, this was a woman who'd dabbled in the seedier side of photography and who openly admitted she was being blackmailed.

But what *hadn't* she told him?

"You're welcome," he said at last. His next pause was long enough for him to see uncertainty grow in her eyes. "When you were down there, did you look around your room?"

Hesitantly, she nodded.

"See anything missing? Anything you recall, offhand, that was gone?"

A tiny frown creased her lovely forehead. "I don't know. No, I can't think of anything."

"That's what I thought."

He noticed her expression was wary as he approached and took the chair beside hers. "In fact, Sydney, it didn't look to me as though *anything* was taken."

"What?"

"Clothes, hair dryer, camera, luggage, even this." He pulled three two-dollar chips and a twenty-dollar bill out of his pocket and handed them to her. "Not many thieves leave behind cold hard cash. Even twenty dollars."

Sydney stared at the chips as though she'd never seen them before. When she raised her face, there was a question in her eyes. "What are you saying, Jack?"

"Don't you think it's a bit strange that someone should rob you but not take anything?"

"Yes, I think that's really weird." She turned the chips over in her fingers. "So, are you saying that someone just vandalized my room for the fun of it?"

"No. That doesn't make sense, either. Out of all the rooms in the Sunburst, why pick yours? And the sort of person who vandalizes probably wouldn't pass up money." He was going to have to ask her about this. Something just didn't sit right with him, and he had to ask. He just wasn't sure he wanted to know.

"I think someone was searching your room." He gave her a long, deliberate look. "What were they searching for, Sydney?"

Startled, she stared at him, not speaking.

"It was done very systematically. Very thoroughly. Whoever it was, they were determined, they were professional and they knew what they were looking for."

She shook her head. "I don't know."

Jack's mouth hardened. "All right. If that's the way you want to play it."

Affronted, she gasped, "Wait a minute. I *don't* know. It doesn't make sense to me, either. I don't have anything anyone would want. My camera maybe, but they didn't take that. Nobody could have possibly known I had ten thousand dollars on me."

"Except the person *blackmailing* you," Jack said.

She gazed at him, suddenly hurt. "Why did you say it like that? Like you don't believe me?"

"Oh, I believe you. I believe that everything you told me is the truth. I just wonder about the parts you haven't mentioned."

When she dropped her gaze to her hands, Jack's heart sank. So, he'd been right. There was more to her story than she'd let on. The thought that she hadn't trusted him enough to tell him the truth caused a slow, dull ache in his chest.

"I've told you the whole story," she mumbled indistinctly.

"Uh-huh."

When she glanced up at him, her blue eyes were troubled. "Really."

"And I'm an Arab sheikh. Come on, Sydney. Don't try to con a con."

He saw her bite her lip, hesitate, then frown.

"Maybe I didn't tell you everything," she said, an appeal in her voice. "But I told you *almost* everything, and the parts I didn't mention aren't that important."

"If they're not important, then it shouldn't bother you to tell me what they are."

Again, her gaze was downcast. "I . . . I can't. I wish I could. I really do. But I . . . I just can't."

"Fine." Although his legs felt heavy and a hollow, burning lump seemed to have developed under his sternum, Jack rose rapidly to his feet and nodded sharply at her. "You can stay here, of course. You know where the guest room is. I'll see you in the morning."

"Jack—"

Raising a hand, he stopped her. "It's all right, Sydney. You don't owe me anything. Certainly not an explanation. I apologize for probing."

At the door to his bedroom, he looked back and saw her sitting exactly as he had left her.

"However," he called and saw her head lift, "if you change your mind about talking, you know where to find me."

Quietly, he shut the bedroom door.

For a long time, Sydney stood in the darkness of the living room. The silence in the suite was so deep and unbroken that she could hardly believe a busy casino was still operating at full capacity just ten floors below. In the quiet night, it seemed to her that she must be the only person awake in the world.

Finally, tightening the belt of the thick terry-cloth robe she'd found hanging behind the bathroom door in the guest room, she swallowed hard, reached for the handle, and pushed open the door to Jack's room.

The bedroom was hushed. Long, heavy drapes had been drawn over the windows, leaving only a thin sliver of light to fall across the thick carpeting. From where she stood, she could faintly discern the bed and the shape of Jack's sleeping form under the sheet. He didn't stir. Soundlessly, she crossed the floor and paused beside him.

She considered perching on the edge of the mattress, then hastily changed her mind and took a seat in a cushioned chair under the windows. From where she was sitting, she could make out his face, dark and shadowy against the white of the pillowcase, and the muscular arm he'd flung out across the top of the sheet.

She knew that sooner or later she would have to wake him. What she'd come to tell him was too important to wait. Still, she was reluctant to disturb him just yet.

Instead, she sat and watched him in silence. He slept on his stomach, his face turned to her. As she watched, she began to notice the rhythmic rise and fall of his broad, bare back with each breath he took. Unconsciously, she began to breathe in unison with him.

For some reason, he looked even bigger in the bed. Her eyes soon grew accustomed to the faint light and she took in more and more details of his body—the way his neck corded, the muscles bunching at the base near his shoulders. She noticed the faint, dark outline of his beard, and the muscles in his wrist and forearm, sturdy and thick like a workman's, yet exquisitely defined under brown skin sprinkled with black hairs.

Even his hands, she thought, were irresistibly masculine. Broad and capable-looking, they had a strength and roughness her own pale, slender fingers did not.

As she studied him, the stillness of the night and the peaceful measure of his steady breathing began to lull her into a dreamy state. She was just imagining what it would be like to run her fingertips down the groove of his spine, when he suddenly spoke.

"Did you come in here to say something, or are you just going to watch me all night?"

Like an electric shock, his voice jolted her from her daydream.

"You're awake," she said inanely.

Rolling onto his side, Jack leaned his elbow on the pillow, rested his cheek against his closed fist and gave her a very alert look. "I haven't been asleep," he said. "Just when I was about to nod off, I heard the sound of little footsteps in my room."

"You've been awake the whole time?"

"I have." He gave her a mischievous smile. "Why are you sitting over there? It's much warmer here in bed."

Feeling foolish at being caught studying him and a little alarmed at the thought of following his suggestion, Sydney struggled with a reply. "I'm not cold."

"Well, then, it's more comfortable over here."

"Jack—"

"There's plenty of room. I'll even share my side of the bed with you."

"I didn't come in here to... What I mean is, I want to tell you something." Unhappily, she paused. "I want to explain."

"Well, good. I was hoping you were going to tell me what's been going on. But you could explain to me from over here, couldn't you?"

"Jack!" She forced herself to take a steadying breath. "Would you please just shut up a minute? I want to talk to you, but not about that. It's about me."

At the unexpectedly raw note of pain in her voice, the teasing light in his eyes faded and his face grew serious. "All right. What is it? What's wrong?"

"Everything's wrong," she moaned, then shook herself. This wasn't the way she wanted it to be. She wanted to be cool and unemotional. With an effort, she made herself say bluntly, "I used to be fat. Did you know that?"

"Fat?" He smiled. "Every woman thinks she's overweight."

"Not overweight. I was fat. Really fat."

For a long moment, he said nothing, his expression thoughtful. "All right," he finally said. "But you're not overweight now. You're gorgeous. You must know you are."

Sydney shook her head. "When I first left home, I thought I would be a famous photographer by the end of the year. But all that happened was that I nearly starved to death. Try eating peanut butter sandwiches every day for two years straight and you'd lose weight, too. But I was always fat."

Jack shrugged. "Some of the most beautiful, charming women I've ever known were technically overweight."

She gave him a barely tolerant look. "That's just what I'm trying to say. Some people are fat, and some are overweight. It's not the same thing at all. I know all about that attitude stuff, and I'm telling you I was *fat*. The thing is, some fat people are always fat. Do you understand? Even when they're skinny, they're fat. They *feel* fat."

Even in the dark, she could see his eyes had grown concerned. "And that's the way you feel?"

Slowly, she nodded. "It's who I am, Jack. It's who I really am inside." She paused again, but only briefly. What she wanted to tell him was so difficult, she'd never told anyone else before. If she hesitated now, she might never be able to say it. "I don't know if you can imagine what it was like, being the fat kid at school. It wasn't fun. I guess that sounds like self-pity, but take my word for it, being fat was hard."

"I'm sure it was, Sydney. But most people have bad things happen to them in their childhoods. You can't let that affect who you are as an adult."

Her gaze on him was steady, though she had begun to tremble very slightly. "You think so? When I was young, everyone compared me to my sister, Sheila, who truly is a knockout. That wasn't so bad because I've always been proud of her. It's just..." For a moment, the memory came rushing back, a ghost of pain from the past, almost choking her. Gripping her hands together tightly, she willed herself to ignore it. "One time, the captain of the football team, Eric Fallows, asked me out. I was surprised. I thought it was a joke. But he kept asking and asking, and finally I agreed. I was young, and I guess I wanted to believe."

"What happened?" Jack had sat up, which pulled him back into the shadows. She couldn't see his face, but his voice sounded low and strangled.

She offered him the bravest, lightest smile she could muster. "Well, I was right. It was a trick. He dumped me off miles from home, at a park where a lot of the popular kids hung out. The rest of the football team was there. I guess, compared to some of the things that happen these days, I got off easy. They only teased me and pushed me around a little. Then, they tied a huge pair of old lady's underpants to the antennae of Eric's car and drove around downtown saying they were mine."

She was staring at her hands, clutched in her lap. She looked up sharply when she heard the bed squeak.

He had swung his legs over the side to sit on the edge of the mattress. Still wearing only a pair of pajama bottoms, he looked large and dark and muscular. Slowly, as though being careful not to startle her, he leaned toward her.

"I'm sorry, Sydney," he said, and sounded as if he meant it. "An experience like that would be horrible for anyone. At that age, it must have been a nightmare for you."

With forced nonchalance, she answered, "Yeah. I guess." Then before he could comment, she added, "So, do you see now what I was trying to tell you earlier tonight? The Sydney Stone you see isn't the real one, Jack. Maybe because, that night, I finally accepted who I really am. I stopped wanting to be anything different. The real Syd is inside, Jack, and she's not pretty or glamorous or any of those things. I can never be those things. I don't even want to be them."

When he reached for her hand, holding it gently, she didn't resist. There was something so comforting in the gesture, she felt her throat tighten.

"You're wrong, Sydney. No matter what you say, you're beautiful. You're beautiful inside and out. The Sydney Stone I know is bright and funny and caring. She's beautiful."

Vehemently, she shook her head. "No. No, I'm not. You just believe that because you want to. Because you don't really know me."

He held her fingers lightly, as though her hand were a delicate bird he was cradling in his palm. With surprise, she felt hard, leathery calluses across his palm.

"Sydney," he said urgently, "when are you going to stop being so afraid?"

Dumbfounded, she stared at him, as surprised as if he had just slapped her. Then abruptly, she pulled her hand from his and turned her face to avoid his searching eyes. "I already told you. I'm *not* afraid. For heaven's sake, Jack. I'm trying to explain to you who I am. Facing reality is not being afraid.''

"But you aren't facing reality. No matter what happened to you when you were young, the reality now is that you're beautiful. You're gorgeous. You're also smart and witty, and you have a strength in you that other people can only envy. *That's* the reality, and maybe it's time you stopped and considered why you won't accept it. Maybe it's time you thought about that.''

She gave him a small, tight smile, hurt that he could discount so easily what had been so difficult for her to confess. "Why should I bother? I'm sure you're going to tell me, yourself, in a minute.''

Jack's eyes narrowed and his mouth hardened at the sarcasm in her voice. For an instant, she almost thought he might shake her. Then closing his eyes and tilting his head, he inhaled deeply before turning back to her.

"Yes, I'm going to tell you. It's time someone did. You *are* afraid, Sydney. That's why you prefer to live a lie. It's easier for you to tell yourself you're plain and uninteresting and dull. And I think I know why. I think it's easier for you because then you don't have to live up to anything. If you told yourself the truth—if you told yourself you're beautiful and intelligent and capable—well, you'd have to do something about it, wouldn't you?''

Sydney gaped at him, not sure if she was staggered because his words were so brutal or because she sensed a grain of truth in them.

"Your problem isn't that you're fat or worthless or weak," he went on. "Your problem is that you're afraid *not* to be those things. You're afraid to try because you're afraid of being disappointed again. Well, Sydney, if I have anything to say about it, that's going to change.''

His eyes were intense and dark, so dark they looked black, and he had leaned forward until she could almost see her reflection in their inky depths.

**IT'S FUN!**

**IT'S FREE!**

## BIG BUCKS

### HOW TO PLAY

It's so easy...grab a lucky coin, and go right to your BIG BUCKS game card. Scratch off silver squares in a STRAIGHT LINE (across, down, or diagonal) until 5 dollar signs are revealed. BINGO!...Doing this makes you eligible for a chance to win $1,000,000.00 in lifetime income ($33,333.33 each year for 30 years)! Also scratch all 4 corners to reveal the dollar signs. This entitles you to a chance to win the $50,000.00 Extra Bonus Prize! Void if more than 9 squares scratched off.

Return your game card and we'll assign you a unique Sweepstakes Number, so it's important that your name and address section is completed correctly. This will permit us to identify you and match you with any cash prize rightfully yours! (SEE BACK OF BOOK FOR DETAILS.)

### FREE BOOKS PLUS FREE GIFTS!

At the same time you play your BIG BUCKS game card for BIG CASH PRIZES...scratch the Lucky Charm to receive FOUR FREE

Silhouette Yours Truly™ novels, and a FREE GIFT, TOO! They're totally free, absolutely free with no obligation to buy anything!

These books have a cover price of $3.50 each. But THEY ARE TOTALLY FREE; even the shipping will be at our expense! The Silhouette Reader Service™ is not like some book clubs. You don't have to make any minimum number of purchases–not even one!

The fact is, thousands of readers look forward to receiving four of the best new romance novels every other month and they love our discount prices!

Of course you may play BIG BUCKS for cash prizes alone by not scratching off your Lucky Charm, but why not get everything that we are offering and that you are entitled to! You'll be glad you did.

Offer limited to one per household and not valid to current Silhouette Yours Truly™ subscribers. All orders subject to approval.

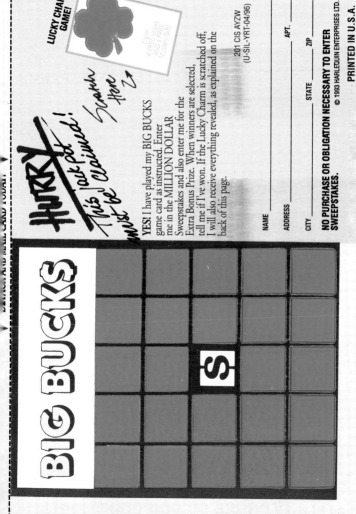

Suddenly, he pulled away from her and put his hands on his knees. "Now, which side of the bed do you want?"

Sydney's mouth nearly fell open. "Which side of the what? You've got to be kidding. You just spent the last few minutes chewing me up and spitting out the pieces."

"Maybe we've discovered a new kind of foreplay?" he suggested, grinning.

"I'm not getting into the same bed with you, Jack Ames." Wounded and angry, Sydney jumped to her feet. "In fact, I don't even want to be in the same *hotel* with you."

Before she could sweep past him, Jack grabbed her wrist with startling quickness. Jerked to a halt, she glared at him.

"Don't check out just yet," he said breezily. "Think about what I said. Really think about it. If you decide I'm way off the mark, well then, I'll apologize. But don't reject out of hand what I said just because it's uncomfortable to admit."

Sydney gritted her teeth. When she'd come to his room to explain, she had expected him to console her. She'd been so certain that he would agree with her and even sympathize. Instead, he'd attacked her. Without knowing exactly why, she felt threatened, even terrified by his suggestions, and her immediate reaction was anger.

"You know what I think? You're mean and arrogant," she retorted. "Arrogant and stuck-up and full of yourself. You think you know everything, Jack? Well, you don't know me. You don't know me at all." Furious, Sydney tugged vainly at her hand. "And let go of my arm. I mean it."

Instead of releasing her, Jack pulled her closer so that her thigh pressed against the hard line of his leg. "I'll admit I'm arrogant, Sydney. From time to time, I might also be a little stuck-up and full of myself, as you say. But I won't agree that I don't know you. Of course, it's true that I don't know everything about you. I'm still learning how that gorgeous, screwy head of yours works. But I *am* learning. Every minute, I'm learning more and more about you. And you know what? The more I learn, the more I find there is to like.''

"You're ridiculous," she said, but most of the anger had gone from her voice. "A real con artist."

He nodded, smiling. "That, too. I admit it. One of the finest once, if I do say so myself."

"Well, it won't work. I know you, too, Jack Ames. After everything you've just said, you can't sweet-talk me."

Pulling her closer still, so that she was pinned between the bed and his leg, he raised an eyebrow. "Frankly, I wasn't planning on doing much talking," he murmured, then casually reached for the belt of her robe.

Like a shot, her hand covered his, stopping him. "Just what do you think you're doing?"

His look was devilish and languid. "I think I'm trying to undress you."

"And I think you'd better stop this nonsense right this minute," she insisted hotly. "Let go of me, Jack."

Despite her clutching fingers, his hand continued to fumble with the sides of the soft robe in an attempt to push them apart. "You're beautiful, Sydney. No matter what you say, that's the truth. Let me show you. Let me prove to you how beautiful you really are."

Sydney dug her nails into the back of Jack's hand, hard. With satisfaction, she felt his fingers pause under hers. "I've been trying to have a serious discussion with you, and all you can do is fool around. Don't you ever think about anything but sex?" she demanded.

"No." His smile was roguish. "Hardly anything else. Not when we're together. Do you?"

The question stopped her. She tried to hold on to her anger, tried to deny the quick and truthful answer that sprang to her lips. Suppressing it, she looked away uncomfortably.

"Of course I do," she muttered. A memory of how she'd wanted, just a few minutes before, to run her hands down the smooth plane of his back made a warm heat rise in her cheeks. Then she realized what she'd just said. Flustered, she tried hurriedly to correct her answer. "I mean, no. I mean, I don't think about it. Sex. I think about other things. I..."

"Uh-huh," he said, amused, as her voice trailed off.

"You know what I mean."

"Oh, yes. I do know." His voice was faintly husky, teasing. "Don't fool yourself, Sydney. I understand more than you think I do. When I touch you, I can feel the shiver on your soft skin. When I get close to you, I can hear your heart beating just a little bit too fast. Sometimes tonight, when I'd look at you, I could see a faint flush creep up your cheeks, just like now, and I know what you're thinking about, Sydney. I know."

She'd gone very still and quiet. Did he know? Could he read her so easily? The thought was a little mortifying.

He was studying her intently, his expression unyielding. "Tell me," he urged. "Tell me the truth this time, Sydney. Do you want to kiss me again? Do you want to kiss me like you did earlier tonight? Because I want to kiss you. I want it more than I've wanted almost anything."

Her throat seemed to have closed up tightly. No words could have passed even if she'd thought of something to say. As though hypnotized, she gazed at him, her eyes trapped by his.

"So, tell me," he continued. "Tell me honestly. If you say no, I'll let you go, and I won't bother you again. I won't try again until you tell me to." His smile was slow and sensual. "But if you say yes, Sydney, you won't regret it. I promise."

Her heart had begun to pound, quick and loud in her ears, and she thought she felt herself sway just the slightest bit.

"Do you want to kiss me?" he repeated, his voice seductive and low.

She was making a mistake. She knew it would be a horrible mistake. He might not believe her, but she knew the truth. She was only playacting, and if she did this, someday she would have to pay the price. When her time here was over and she was back at Little Vernon's Bar and Grill, alone with the long days stretching out empty before her, she would have to pay the price.

Light-headed, dizzy with the rush of longing and dread that washed through her, she told herself to walk away and save herself. Yet his eyes held hers, silently promising—promising everything she'd only dreamed about. For one blinding, shattering moment, she realized the truth. She would give the world, the rest of her life, to kiss him and be held by him just once. No price was too great.

"Yes," she said, so faintly the word was barely a sigh. "I want to kiss you."

# 7

Sydney's words hovered in the silence of the dark bedroom like a wispy mist, light and clinging.

Jack tilted his head inquisitively, a slow smile growing on his lips. "But," he said. "But will you let yourself? That's the question, isn't it? Will you let yourself?"

There was a challenge in his voice and invitation in his eyes. With a start, she realized he knew just what this meant for her. Of course he did. He was a gambler, wasn't he? He understood about chances, about taking risks.

He had said she was afraid, and despite herself, she knew in her heart it was true. For once in her life, she decided suddenly, she didn't want to be afraid. She didn't want to second-guess herself or think about the consequences. For just once in her life, she wanted to be a gambler, too.

Before she could reconsider, Sydney leaned forward and placed a hand on each of his broad shoulders. His bare skin was smooth and firm, warmer than she'd expected. Closing her eyes, she touched her lips to his.

It was a whisper of a kiss, as delicate as a summer breeze. Yet, as her mouth brushed his, the taste of his lips and the feel of his muscles under her hands was like a jolt that sent her senses reeling. At once, she became aware of the heat from his body, the sweet, faint muskiness of his skin and the warmth of his breath. Overwhelmed by sensation, she barely realized when his hands closed around her waist.

As if in a dream, she felt him guide her to the bed beside him. Her hands were around his neck now, and still his lips were on hers, persuading, teasing, exploring. Disoriented, it took her a moment before she realized he had opened her robe and was gently sliding it off her shoulders.

"Jack," she said breathlessly as the robe fell to the bed.

"It's all right. This is what's supposed to happen. What we both want." He placed a finger on her cheek, tracing down to her chin. His eyes seemed to burn blackly, and the fierce desire in his face made her catch her breath. "It's not as much of a gamble as you think it is. I'm not going to leave you in a park, Sydney. I'm not going to leave you anywhere."

She didn't believe him, but suddenly that didn't seem to matter. His finger had trailed to the hollow of her neck and paused on the fluttering pulse there, then continued to the valley between her breasts. A hot, fiery ache leaped alive deep inside her, and Sydney closed her eyes.

When his mouth found hers again, there was a new urgency in his kiss, and her body responded to it as though it had a will of its own. Clinging to his shoulders, she returned his kisses eagerly, full of wonder and delight at the prickling of his beard against her skin and the hot pressure of his lips against hers.

When his hand strayed down to cup her breast in one large palm, she heard him moan.

"God, you're beautiful, Sydney. So soft and so silky. All luscious curves and sweet honey. Lady Luck." He raised his head to smile at her, tangling his fingers in her hair and tilting her head back to hold her gaze with his. "Tonight, Lady Luck is mine."

"Yours." She'd meant it to be a question, but it didn't come out that way.

For one brief moment, she thought she saw a glimmer of triumph in his eyes, but it was gone so quickly she wondered if she'd misread it. She knew only that she wanted him.

When he laid them down on top of the rumpled sheets, kicking off his pajama bottoms and stretching out beside her, she nestled against him and buried her face in the crook of his neck. The first feel of his hot skin against hers nearly took her breath away. Strong arms drew her closer still, as though he wanted to mold them together. Tentatively at first, then with growing ardor, she ran her hand over the hard contours of his body, the swell of steely muscles in his arms and the solid, rigid lines of his broad chest, dusted with black curly hairs that tickled her palm.

Yet, when he slid a hand to the small of her back and she felt him press a heavy, muscled thigh between her knees, a sudden, nameless panic made her stiffen and freeze.

Instantly, Jack paused and raised his head to meet her eyes. His face was dark and tense with arousal, and a muscle in his jaw jumped as he clenched his teeth.

"What is it?" he asked, his voice thick and a little hoarse. "What's wrong?"

"I..." She ran the tip of her tongue over her lip. "It's been a long time for me, Jack."

His face relaxed, and his smile was knowing. "Yes, I know. I guessed as much."

His powerful hand, fanned across the small of her back, resumed its pressure. Effortlessly, he drew her closer, sliding his leg between her thighs.

Sydney clamped her legs around his leg, stopping him, and placed her hands firmly on his chest. "Jack. It's been a *long* time," she repeated.

"I know," he said, raising himself. As easily as if she were a child, he eased her onto her back. Leaning on one elbow, he hung over her. "Look at me, Sydney."

For a moment, she pretended not to hear him, then gradually she opened her eyes. His face was intent and almost strained, as though he was struggling to maintain control.

"I want to make love to you, Sydney. I want to show you just how very beautiful you are. I would never do anything to hurt or frighten you. Never. Do you understand that?"

"Yes, I know," she whispered. "But what if you can't help it?"

Surprise flickered in his dark eyes. "What do you mean? I don't understand."

"Well, isn't there kind of a point where you..." Her voice trailed off, then she began again, "Well, not just you. I mean, men. Isn't there this point where you, well, sort of just can't help yourselves? You know."

The bewilderment on his face was replaced by stony dismay. "No, there is not," he said roughly. "Who in the world ever told you that?"

With a pained expression, Sydney recalled the young art student she'd met at a Venice art gallery years ago and the clumsy, awkward fumblings they'd shared on the beach that summer. But before she could open her mouth to reply, Jack laid a finger across her lips.

"Never mind," he said, a strange, cold glint in his eyes she'd never seen there before. "I don't want to know."

As if it was an effort not to say more, he closed his eyes and turned his head away. The muscles in his neck stood out, corded and taut. When he finally looked at her again, his eyes were gentle and he was smiling tenderly.

"If there is ever a time when I can't help myself, believe me, it'll be because that's what you want. You don't have to be afraid of making love, Sydney. Not with me. When I touch you," he said, laying a finger on the sensitive skin of her cleavage, "it's because I want to hear you sigh."

Steadily, unhurriedly, his finger traced the hollow, then the curve beneath her breast, and Sydney had to hold back the sudden sigh that rose in her throat.

"When I kiss you," he murmured, lowering his mouth to her breast, "it's to hear you moan."

With excruciating lightness, she felt his tongue flick across her nipple, and her blood quickened. Before she could help herself, a tiny moan escaped her lips. At the sound, he raised his head, a languid smile growing on his face.

"When I hold you," he said, his voice huskier now, "it's to show you how beautiful you are. Look, Sydney," he commanded. "Look at how beautiful you are."

Helplessly, she obeyed, peering at her own white breast, cupped in his rough, tanned hand. The sight was startling and achingly sensual. It *was* beautiful, she thought. Against the dark, granite lines of his large body, her own body looked soft and pale and small. Beside him, she *did* look beautiful.

Slowly, lingeringly, his fingers wandered under her breast and down her ribs, circling and caressing. His touch was as light as a feather and as tormentingly erotic as nothing she had ever known before.

"And when we come together," he said, holding her gaze with his as his hand trailed to the patch of golden-brown hair between her legs. "And when we come together," he repeated, "it'll be because that's what you want."

When his fingers slipped gently into the tender folds, she heard herself inhale sharply. Instinctively, she tried to close her legs, but his hard-muscled thigh was there, holding her open to his touch.

"I think," she whispered weakly, "you've made your point."

His eyes had grown dusky and shadowed. "Oh, no," he protested, lowering his face once more to her breast and circling the nipple with his tongue. "No, I haven't even started yet."

Softly, slowly, his fingers parted her, and Sydney felt herself growing wetter and more excited. The deep, throbbing ache in her swelled, threatening to devour her, and when he slid a finger inside her, she gasped and reached for his forearm beside her head, gripping it.

"I meant, I already do," she managed to say in a rush. "That *is* what I want."

His teeth grazed lightly over her nipple. Raising his head only briefly, he smiled at her.

"I know," he said, his voice low and ragged. "You're so wet and warm and tight. I know you want it, but there's no rush. We've got all night. You're small, Sydney, and I don't want to hurt you."

He was touching her more intimately, more sensuously than anyone had ever touched her before. She felt the ache in her grow warmer, until she seemed on fire. Burning, smoldering embers melted her flesh.

"I don't care," she moaned. Unable to help herself, she began to move, twisting under his teasing mouth and practiced hands. "I don't care if it hurts."

Raising his head from her breast, he covered her mouth with his, as though capturing the small, breathless moans she made.

"But I care," he murmured against her lips.

With agonizing deliberation, he eased a second finger inside her, tantalizing and teasing with his hands as surely as he seduced her lips with his. Persistent and coaxing, his kiss was like a promise, urging her to a new state of passion and encouraging the fire that was blazing in her, hot and searing.

"Jack," she cried softly as the ache began to burn more fiercely.

From very far away, she heard Jack's voice, reassuring. "I'm here, Sydney. I'm here, sweetheart."

With a suddenness that took her breath away, the flames exploded, consuming her, and she grasped blindly for him, clinging to his shoulders as wave after wave swept through her.

The whole world seemed to stop, suspended, leaving only the glorious rush of fire beating and pulsing through her. Gradually, she became aware of her own voice, crying Jack's name in a strangely hollow tone.

Then he was kissing her, his mouth on hers more fierce and demanding than before. Spreading her legs wider with his thigh, he raised himself on his arms and settled over her. She could feel his manhood, thick and jutting, against her stomach, and she pulled at his shoulders to bring him closer to her, but he resisted. Looming over her, every muscle in his body taut and strained, he gazed into her eyes.

"What do you want, Sydney?" he asked in almost a groan.

"I want you," she breathed. "I want you inside me."

His broad chest heaved with each breath he took. "Then put me there," he whispered.

She hesitated, but the flesh of her body—softened and melted by his touch—cried out for more, craving more. Slowly, she moved her hand from his shoulder and down the ridged plane of his stomach to the large, heavy shaft. Hard as stone, yet covered in velvety soft skin, she closed her hand around him and heard him moan.

Tilting back his head so that the muscles in his neck and chest stood out, he closed his eyes and clamped his teeth. Fascinated and in awe at this unknown power she sensed she had over him, she touched him lightly, exploratively, and his answering response was a tortured groan.

"You want to kill me," he gasped. "Well, go ahead."

"I just want to touch you, too," she said, and gently stroked him.

"Sydney." The ragged cry was dragged from his throat.

"I guess you can't take your own medicine," she teased, and guided him with her hand to the dark opening between her legs.

At the first thrust, her body resisted, unyielding, and she stiffened in a sudden, instinctive response to his invasion. Very carefully, he lowered himself over her, resting his weight on one elbow, and drew her leg up and around him.

"Raise your legs, sweetheart," he murmured. "Yes, around me like that."

The next push made her gasp and clutch at his shoulders, and she tensed against him. Softly, with infinite gentleness, he stroked her hip and the tender skin on the inside of her thigh, slowly easing himself into her.

The fire was starting again, and with each plunge, her body relented, softening and melding with his until there was only the hushed, rhythmic rise and fall of his body on hers, his body in hers, his body becoming hers.

Like drops of dew, he rained tiny kisses on her face and throat as his breath came quick and harsh, and the heat in her spread like wildfire.

"Oh, Sydney," he cried, his body tensing under her hands like a bow.

He was filling her, lovely and full, and she raised her hips to meet him, wanting more. Each stroke seemed to fuel the fire, and this time she wanted to burn. She craved it, longed for it. When she felt the flames roar up, she heard herself cry out, just as he gave a jagged, broken shout. Then all was silent, but for the rush and roar of the inferno sweeping her away.

Kicking the door shut with his foot, Jack returned to the bedroom carrying a tray laden with leftovers from their late supper. Setting it on a corner of the bed, he stretched out beside her, tugging away the sheet from under her chin and kissing her before she could snatch it up again.

She was exquisite, Jack thought, moving the sheet aside still farther to reveal her tantalizing nakedness underneath. In the dim light of the bedside lamp, her skin looked as pale and smooth as marble and her breasts were round and heavy, the rosy pink buds of her nipples perky and just visible over the arms she crossed in front of her.

Like the Venus de Milo, which he had once seen in the Louvre years ago, her generous curves were full and voluptuous and, oh so womanly. Yet unlike that enchanting statue, her flesh was real and flushed with the bloom of life and the lingering effects of their lovemaking.

The thought that he had made her look like that—soft and drowsy with pleasure—delighted him, and he was contemplating starting all over again, when a glass toppled over on the tray at their feet.

Her eyes were smoky. "I thought you said you were hungry."

"I am." Nuzzling her breast, he pretended to take a bite. "Funny thing about making love with you, Sydney. It just seems to whet my appetite for more."

"You *said* you were hungry for lobster."

"Did I? Hmm. I don't usually make mistakes like that." Pulling himself up and crossing his legs under him, he grinned at her. "Are you *sure* I didn't say for you?"

"I'm sure. I'd remember something like that." Leaning forward so that he got a heady, tantalizing glimpse of her soft, rounded bottom, she slid the tray across the bed toward them. "Champagne?" she exclaimed in surprise. "But it's four in the morning."

"It is? That's wonderful. It's the champagne hour then."

Laughing, she watched him pour, then took a glass of the bubbly wine from him. "I never drank champagne in bed before."

"No! Good God. Well, don't worry, it's not too late. We'll have to concentrate, but I'm sure we can catch you up on that." Popping a piece of lobster into his mouth, Jack sighed and licked his fingers. "Mmm. Perfect. Here, you've got to try this."

Obediently she opened her mouth and took the morsel of tender white lobster from his fingers. Deliberately, she ran the tip of her tongue slowly, sensually, over her lips.

"You're right," she said, laughing softly. "That's really good."

"Uh-huh." With a look of mock severity, he scooped caviar onto a cracker. "Don't tempt me much more, or we'll both be wearing caviar and lobster in the morning."

"Really? I've never done that, either." Her tone suggested she wouldn't mind trying.

Jack raised his eyebrows. "Little tease." Bringing another bite of lobster to her luscious, shell-pink lips, he watched her take it from him and his stomach tightened. "I think your opinion of my willpower is highly overestimated."

"Oh, I don't know. You seem to be pretty much in control," she said, accepting a cracker from him. She shot a quicksilver smile at him. "At least, most of the time."

"Eat your cracker. Before I ravish you."

She laughed aloud and something in his heart melted. He could sense the joy in her, as though she were a child who'd found a wonderful, new game. Before his eyes, she was blossoming, exploring the uncharted territories of her own femininity. Her elation at her power was evident in every aspect of her beautiful face, and he was thrilled at the sight of her wonderment.

Under his rapt, almost dreamy gaze, she had grown still. Glancing down at the cracker he'd handed her, she raised it to her lips, then lowered her hand without taking a bite.

"Jack?"

"Hmm?" he replied, imagining how it would feel to trace the line of her breast with his finger.

"Can I ask you something?"

"Of course." Sitting back, he smiled at her. "Ask away."

Once again, she looked down at the cracker she was holding, then set it on the tray untasted. "Who are you, Jack? I mean, where are you from? I don't really know anything about you."

"You know the most important things. After tonight, I'd say you knew me pretty well."

"But I don't. Not really. I don't even know if you have a family or where you live."

"Is that important?"

A thoughtful frown creased her forehead. "I'm not sure whether it is or not. I just know I want to know about you. I want to know where you've been and how you got to be so comfortable with... with this sort of life. Everything."

Jack looked away, considering, then leaned back against the pillows, stretching out his legs. From the nightstand, he took a cigarette, lit it with a gold lighter and exhaled thoughtfully.

"All right," he said. "You want to know about me. Where should I start?"

"How about where you're from? Where did you grow up?"

"Everywhere." He put an arm behind his head. "All over the world. My father was in the foreign service."

"The foreign service?"

"The Brits' version of the diplomatic corps."

"Your father's British?"

Jack nodded. "My mother was an American. She left when I was still young. Couldn't take the heat in Morocco, Dad always said."

"I'm sorry."

He shrugged. "Don't be. My childhood was anything but unhappy, believe me. In some ways, it was a wonderful life for a child."

She was studying him, nodding as though he'd confirmed her ideas. "You know, I thought you had a bit of an accent." She smiled. "A sort of 'Masterpiece Theater' accent."

"Oh, God." He groaned melodramatically. "Don't say that. I spent years trying to get rid of it. When I was a kid, I wanted to be an American. Most of the Brits I knew were so deadly dull. Humphrey Bogart, James Dean—those were my idols. I spent my whole tenth year saying, 'Here's looking at you, kid' to every guest who ever visited the house, until Dad threatened to cut off my allowance. I even talked him into sending me to school here in the States. For a while."

Her blue eyes had clouded slightly. "Was it," she began, "because of your mother? That you wanted to be an American, I mean."

Her question made him pause, but only for a moment. "Maybe. Maybe, it was."

Silently, she watched him, waiting. When he didn't elaborate, she asked, "So, how did you get started? How did you get involved in gambling?"

"And theft and cons," he added for her, then shrugged. "Because it was exciting."

"Exciting?"

Stubbing out his cigarette, he gave her a long look. "Yes, exciting. That's all there is to it. I wish I had a better excuse. But the truth is, I was simply young and too daring for my own good. I did it because it was thrilling. You see, with the way I'd grown up, by twenty I felt I'd done everything there was to do and seen everything there was to see. Then I met Frenchie in Monte Carlo. We got along. He showed me the ropes, and I got hooked. One thing just led to another."

"You were only twenty?"

"Around there, yes." He smiled a little ruefully. "It's not a very pretty story, I know. But there was something about it—the rush of adrenaline, the cold bite of fear before we pulled a job—that was intoxicating. The knot in the pit of your stomach when you've got fifty thousand dollars riding on just one roll of the dice, the heady triumph when your mark suddenly takes the bait—it was exhilarating. Like a drug you can't get enough of. And then, of course—"

He broke off, leaving the last thought unfinished. After a few moments, Sydney asked, "Are you sorry you did it? I mean, you sound like maybe you are."

"I suppose I am. We never endangered anyone. And we never hit any mark that wasn't wealthy enough to easily stand the loss. Still, it's not the sort of life I'd recommend to anyone. There are a lot of unsavory characters out there. It does something to your psyche to think you might be one of them."

"Then why did you keep doing it?"

Jack was quiet, remembering. At last, he said softly, "Because I couldn't let Frenchie go it alone. He needed me. He was getting older, and I was worried he might make a mistake. Slip up and hurt someone. Or himself. Well, I was right. He did hurt someone. But I couldn't do anything about it.''

"I see." Sydney, too, was silent for a long moment. "So once he died, you quit."

Jack felt a pang of the old grief, but fought off the memory of that terrible night. "Yes," he said quietly. "I quit. Frenchie didn't need me anymore, at any rate."

"Are you . . . are you sure you don't miss it?"

The thin note of trepidation in her voice made him smile.

"Not really. Occasionally, I miss the excitement, but never for very long. The trouble with that kind of excitement is that it doesn't last. A few hours, a few days later, and you have to go back for more." Abruptly sitting up, he reached out and touched the silky skin of her cheek. "I'm older now and, I hope, a little wiser. I've learned that the quick fix doesn't really satisfy. I prefer other, longer-term pleasures now."

Under his caress, her face flushed a becoming pink.

"So now that I've told you everything," he said softly, "shouldn't it be your turn next?"

At his words, she suddenly went still, almost rigid.

"Tell me what's going on, Sydney," he urged. "You know you can trust me. I can help you, if only you tell me what's going on."

Her eyes were turned from him, and he saw her swallow hard.

"I don't know what you mean," she said, her voice a shade too bright. "I told you all about myself. What there is to know."

"That's not what I'm talking about, and you know it." Despite his words, his voice was gentle. "You're in some sort of trouble that you haven't told me about yet. People don't get their rooms searched for no reason. Does this have to do with, well, with the photographs? With the blackmailer?"

She shook her head. "No. No, it doesn't. How many times do I have to tell you? I don't *know* why someone would break into my room. I don't know what anyone could want of mine." Finally, she looked at him, her expression beseeching. "I'm telling you the truth."

"But there are things you haven't told me," he insisted. "You said so yourself earlier tonight. Is it about the blackmailer? Because I want you to know that, no matter what you might have done in the past, it doesn't matter to me, Sydney. I can take care of this creep. I can take care of this problem for you. But you've got to talk to me."

"Jack, please," she protested.

Suddenly feeling hurt, he dropped his hand. "Why, Sydney? Just tell me that. I'd say you were bright and about as stubborn as hell. So, how did this slime bag talk you into doing something like that? Is that what you're worried about? Is that why you won't talk to me? Did he make you do something you can't—"

"Stop it." Rising to her knees, she covered her ears and scrunched her eyes closed. "Just stop it, Jack. I can't talk about it. Please, please, try to understand. I just can't talk about it."

Startled at the intensity of her outcry, he stared at her.

"I would tell you everything if I could," she went on, her voice rising. "I swear I would. Oh, God, what a mess. I know this doesn't make sense, but it doesn't really have anything to do with me. Would you just try to believe that?"

"Doesn't have anything to do with you?" he exclaimed. "Are you serious? Someone just ransacked your room. If that's an example of nothing to do with you, then I'd like to know what is."

"Jack, please."

He could feel himself tensing with frustration and anger. In vain, he stared at her, willing her to trust him, to open up to him. Yet on her troubled face was a belligerence he was beginning to recognize.

Abruptly, he fell back against the pillows again. "Hell," he cursed. "Bloody hell, Sydney."

She glanced at him warily, then a tiny smile lifted one corner of her mouth. "Your accent's showing," she said, her voice uncertain.

Jack ground his teeth, then suddenly felt a smile touch his own lips. "You're going to drive me crazy," he said roughly. "I can tell already. By the time you get done with me, I'll be lucky if I can speak at all."

Slowly, almost cautiously, she crept up the bed toward him. "Somehow, I doubt that, Jack. I really do."

## 8

For the rest of the night, Sydney lay awake, watching the sleeping man on the bed beside her, wondering what terrible things he might be imagining about her and cursing the loyalty that prevented her from telling him about her sister. It was horribly ironic that the one piece of information that could ease Jack's mind, that could prove to him she trusted him completely, was the one thing she couldn't tell him.

For a moment that night—for just the slightest moment—she'd almost confessed the truth to him. Then she'd remembered her promise to Sheila, who'd made her swear not to breathe a word to anyone. Despite her sister's faults, Sheila's fears about her reputation were not entirely unfounded.

It was the thought of Sheila, frightened and at the mercy of a blackmailer, that finally stilled her tongue. No matter what Jack thought of her, she had to protect her sister. It was her first responsibility, as it had always been.

Worried and astonished at the new turn events had taken, it wasn't until almost dawn that Sydney finally dozed off. When she did, the sleep she fell into was deep and exhausted.

It was late in the morning when Claus woke her, laying a breakfast tray on the nightstand as if it was the most natural thing in the world. Dazed and sleepy, Sydney sat up and gazed at the empty space beside her.

"Where's Jack?" she asked, blushing as she pulled the sheet up to her chin.

Just turning to leave, Claus paused. "'Morning, Miss Sydney. Mr. Ames went out a couple hours ago."

"He did?"

Claus hesitated. "I went down and got your stuff, Miss Sydney. You want me to bring it in?"

"My stuff?"

"From your old room. Not much left. Most of your clothes were ruined."

"Oh. Jack told you about last night?"

"Sure. He already talked to the hotel. You're going to stay with us now."

Sydney stared at him. "I'm what?"

"And Mr. Ames said to take you shopping. Till he gets back." Claus started for the door. "I'll bring your stuff now."

"Wait, Claus," she called.

"Yes, Miss Sydney?"

"Do you . . . do you think I could make a long-distance call?" she asked, then added quickly in case he wondered, "To my sister."

As soon as she'd explained, she wished she hadn't. Explaining only made her request sound suspicious, and the less anyone thought of her sister, the better.

"Sure. Mr. Ames won't mind."

"Thanks." Picking up the receiver on the night table, Sydney started to dial, then stopped abruptly. "What do you mean, take me shopping?" she called, but Claus had already left, shutting the door behind him with a click.

Sydney spent the rest of the morning being bullied by Claus and going from one store to another where he made her try on outfit after outfit, brandishing Jack's credit cards like a sacred talisman. After he'd exhausted the salespeople in the ground-floor boutiques of the Sunburst, he ordered

Jack's rented limousine and happily dragged her through a dozen more shops up and down the Strip.

Even the thrill of riding in the luxurious limo with its white-leather seats and fold-down bar, its television and phone, couldn't displace the uneasiness she felt. She didn't really blame Jack for being so upset with her last night. Obviously he was hurt and thought she didn't trust him. She just wished she didn't care as much as she did—which was, she thought, a lot like wishing the moon was made of green cheese.

If only she could have talked to Sheila about this dilemma. But although she'd gotten through to her sister's house, Sheila hadn't been home. Reluctantly, Sydney had left a message saying that everything was fine, that she'd taken care of the problem and that she'd call again later.

Her one, harmless night of glamor, Sydney thought as she wriggled and squirmed into yet another short skirt behind a dressing-room door, was turning into a dangerous, confusing game of passions that could only lead to trouble—the kind of trouble a person didn't get over very quickly.

Perspiration ran in rivulets down his face and his muscles burned, but Jack continued to pull at the handles of the rowing machine, forcing his body to accomplish what his mind could not. After jogging on the hotel gym's treadmill for forty-five minutes, he soaked in the Jaccuzi for just five minutes, when an imaginary pair of candid blue eyes stung him into another frustrated bout with the punching bag.

No matter how hard he worked, he couldn't seem to dislodge the knot of frustration in his chest. Last night, he knew, he'd come dangerously close to falling in love with Sydney Stone. Perhaps he had even done more than come close. Yet, although he wanted to revel in the unexpectedly momentous and passionate bond they'd begun to forge, he was filled instead with foreboding and misgivings.

What wasn't she telling him? he asked himself for the hundredth time. And why couldn't she?

That last question, he knew, was the most important. Sydney was in trouble. That was obvious enough. But had she maintained her silence because she didn't want to involve him? Or was it something worse? Could it be that she had her own agenda? Was she not merely holding something back, but actually deceiving him?

Again he thought of the way they'd met. The chance encounter—"coincidence," she'd called it. But had it been?

Jack hit the bag with a well-placed kick from the side of his foot, pivoted, hit with his other foot, then just as quickly struck a final, rapid-fire series of punches with his hands.

It didn't make sense, he told himself again. He knew people. He'd made a fortune out of his ability to read people. And he would stake his life that Sydney was an innocent. That she could be up to something deceptive was just too inconceivable.

Which meant, he concluded as he peeled off his T-shirt, wrapped a towel around his waist and headed for the steam room, that she was in some kind of trouble and was shielding someone.

But who? he wondered, sinking onto a wooden bench and closing his eyes. Himself? The thought was laughable. But if she wasn't trying to protect him, then who?

Lost in thought, Jack didn't hear the soft whooshing of the steam-room door open. With his head resting against the damp tiles and his eyes closed, he didn't notice the two men who silently entered. Perhaps it was premonition or simply blind luck, but his eyes flew open just in time to make out, indistinct in the thick steam, two large figures in street clothes before the first blow to his gut knocked the wind from his body.

Doubling over and instinctively protecting his stomach, he heard the kick before he saw it. Despite the hard workout he'd just put himself through, fear made him quick, and he grabbed the foot before it could connect with the side of his head. Yanking and turning the foot at the same time, he saw the dark, hazy shape of the man topple heavily to the side and heard the loud crack of the man's head hit the tile floor. Even as Jack rose, balancing on the wooden bench and readying himself for the next attack, he winced at the sound.

The second figure hesitated, looking for all the world like a shadowy phantom rising from the mist. The first man lay unmoving on the tiles, and this fact seemed to decide the issue for the second figure.

Edging toward the door, the murky shape paused, and Jack heard a deep, guttural voice growl, "You keep looking over your shoulder, Ames. 'Cause I'm still going to have a little talk with you."

"Talk?" Jack snarled. "That was goddamned *talk* for you gorillas?"

Again the voice came out of the foggy steam. "You're going to see a lot more of it, too."

"What, if you don't mind my asking, was the talk we just had about?"

A low snicker oozed toward him from the door. "Try Mr. Van Hausen's two million dollars. You remember that, don't you?"

The door opened a crack, letting in a cold draft of air. "By the way, chump," the voice added, "he wants it back."

"Sydney," Jack called in a low, ominous voice. "We need to talk."

Just inside the door to the suite, her arms loaded with boxes and bags, Sydney froze. Close behind her, Claus didn't realize she'd paused and nearly bowled her over, sending her armful of boxes cascading to the floor.

"Oops. Sorry." Claus squeezed through the door, similarly burdened with shopping bags. He, too, halted in surprise.

In the middle of the living room, Jack stood, looking grim and as fierce as a Hun. He was wearing a thick, white terrycloth robe, and his hair was wet and messy. A cigarette burned away unnoticed in the ashtray on the table behind him.

"Jack," Sydney began.

"Mr. Ames," Claus said.

With one quietly intimidating word, Jack interrupted them both. "Now," he ordered.

"I better go put these away," Claus muttered.

Sydney gave the big man a sharp look of betrayal as he scurried from the room.

"What," she began nervously, "what's wrong? If you're mad about my going shopping, I didn't want to. Claus said you told him to take me. It's not a problem. I can take everything ba—"

"Sit down."

Biting her lip, Sydney sat. "All right. There's no need to look so mean. What did you want to talk about?"

Jack's smile was wicked. "Oh, I don't know. Let's start with the night we 'accidentally' met. Then we can go on to consider what someone was searching for in your room last night and this story of yours about blackmailers. Finally, we could go on and talk about the two million dollars my old friend Carlton Van Hausen is missing and thinks *I* took."

Sydney stared at him, speechless.

Jack's eyes narrowed. "The order doesn't really matter. Where would *you* like to start?"

"I don't understand."

"I'll bet you don't."

Sydney felt her mouth go a little dry. "Honest. What are you talking about? What two million dollars? I don't know any Carson Van Houston."

Jack gave a quick, unamused smile and shook his head. "Nice, Sydney. Nice touch. You know perfectly well his name's Carlton Van Hausen."

"No, I don't. I've never heard of the guy before."

Jack studied her, and she saw doubt flicker in his eyes. "It just so happens that he owns this place. The hotel. The casino. Everything."

"So?"

"So, two of his goons just had a little 'discussion' with me in the gym's steam room. They wanted to chat about two million dollars of Carlton's money that's gone missing."

"Goons?" she breathed, starting to rise. "Are you all right? Did they hurt you?"

He waved her back to her seat. "No. No, I'm pretty good at talking my way out of things, so to speak. What I want to know is, why are they coming to me about the money?"

"I don't know." She stared at him, then asked faintly, "Did you take it?"

"Did I—" Jack faltered, glaring at her. "Of course I didn't take it. I've done some stupid things in my time, but stealing from one of the biggest casino owners in Vegas is not one of them. Put it this way, it's a little like standing in front of a train and thinking you might catch a ride."

Her eyes widened. "Maybe you should go talk to him," she suggested. "If he's an old friend of yours, he'll probably believe you."

"Look, Sydney," Jack said, sounding as though he was at the end of his tether. "That's not the point. I know I don't have it, and Carlton doesn't give a damn. Not when we're talking about that much cash. The point is, why does he think I'm his man?"

Sydney shook her head.

"Maybe I'm blowing this whole thing way out of proportion," Jack said, his voice suggesting that he was doing nothing of the kind. "But when I came to Las Vegas less than a week ago, I intended to participate in a little innocent gambling and perhaps even relax a bit. Instead, every time I turn around, there are some very unpleasant incidents taking place around me. And nobody seems to want to tell me what's going on."

Again, she shook her head. "I don't know. It doesn't make sense, does it?"

"Oh, really?"

"Well, not to me."

"Then let me put it another way," Jack said. "Since you happened 'quite by chance' to stumble into my life, Sydney, I've made over seven hundred thousand dollars and had a hell of a good time celebrating. I have also been told a story about blackmail, seen your hotel room ripped apart in a frantic search for *something*, been attacked in the steam room without a stitch of clothing, and been accused of stealing two million dollars, an accusation that could very possibly get me killed. All in all, I think I'd rather do without the seven hundred thousand."

Sydney's eyes widened in sudden understanding. "You think *I* took it?" she asked in astonishment.

"The thought had crossed my mind, yes."

"That's ridiculous," she scoffed. Suddenly, she smiled. "Oh, I get it. You're kidding, aren't you? Pulling my leg. There are no goons and no two million. This is your idea of a joke."

"It isn't a joke."

"Come on," she said lightly.

"I'm dead serious, Sydney."

She blinked at him, then glanced around the room as though looking for something. Finally, she turned back to him. "You really mean this."

"I do."

At the grim light in his eyes, a cold shiver fluttered across her skin, and Sydney trembled. "I didn't take that money," she said quietly. "I wouldn't even know how."

He watched her wordlessly.

"You do believe me, don't you?" she asked.

Jack sighed, and his shoulders relaxed a bit. Sinking to a chair, he shook his head repeatedly.

"Talk about luck," he grumbled. "God help me, but I believe you. I don't know why. I should probably have my head examined. But yes, I believe you."

Sydney let out her breath. "Well then, what are we going to do? I mean, if you didn't take it and I didn't take it, who did? And what are we going to do about it?"

"We?"

"Yes, we. You helped me out, Jack, when I needed more money for the blackmailer. I'm not going to chicken out and run when you're in trouble."

For the first time that morning, a genuine, although faint, smile lifted the corners of Jack's mouth. "*We* aren't going to do anything about it. *You* are going to sit tight and stay out of it. *I'm* going to ask around. I'll do some digging on my own and hope Carlton catches the real thief soon...."

"And what if he doesn't? What are our options then? And don't say life-insurance policies."

"*Our* options? You aren't involved in this, Sydney. This is my problem."

"Well, I'm making it my problem, too. So, what are our options?"

Jack couldn't suppress a smile. "How about chicken out and run for it?"

"For the last time," Jack said angrily, throwing open the door to the corridor outside the suite, "you aren't coming with me." And that, he thought, made about as much sense as telling the earth to stop revolving.

Despite his arguments and refusals, Sydney had spent the last half hour wheedling and cajoling, begging to come with him. The woman, he thought in exasperation, just didn't know how to take no for an answer.

Standing in the doorway now, she scowled prettily at him. In a new, decidedly flattering scarlet and white suit that left a good deal of long, silk-clad leg visible, Jack thought she looked luscious enough to eat.

"I'll be quiet. I won't say a word," she coaxed.

"No." Stepping into the hall, he nearly shut the door on her when she slipped out after him. "I said no, Sydney. Would you please get back in the suite?"

Her face was set in stubbornness. Jack sighed.

"Let me come with you," she pleaded. "I won't get in your way. I promise. But if this friend can help you, well, maybe you'll need me, too."

"Sydney, I work best alone. Do you understand?"

She suddenly looked hurt. "I thought you said we were in this together."

"No, I didn't. If I recall correctly, what I said was that *I* was in this, and it was probably all your fault." Out of patience, Jack flung his hands up. "Look, Sydney, I'm not going to discuss this anymore. You aren't coming with me. Can't I make you understand? Carlton isn't the sort of man to play games. He's serious about this. If those two hoods show up again, I don't want you anywhere close to me. Now, please, get back inside."

"If you think something's going to happen, I'm not going to—"

"Claus!" Jack shouted.

Instantly, the big man was at the open door, peering out at them. Obviously he had been hovering nearby, anxious ever since they'd told him what was going on.

"Yes, Mr. Ames?"

"Take her back inside, and lock the door. Don't let anybody in, don't let anybody near her, and for God's sake, don't let her out of your sight."

"Yes, sir." Gently but firmly, Claus closed a hand over Sydney's arm.

"I'll be back in a few hours," Jack said, absently straightening his striped tie and tucking it into the lapels of his dark suit jacket. "I promise. And don't worry. I'll be fine," he added.

But his reassurances went unnoticed. In disgust, she'd already turned her back on him and stomped angrily into the suite.

Behind her, Sydney heard the click of the door as Claus shut and bolted it. Clasping her hands, she thought furiously, and almost out of the blue the idea came to her. Excited, knowing she had to work fast but realizing that what she was about to do would take tact and patience, Sydney slowly turned.

Claus was watching her anxiously, his face unhappy.

"It's okay," she said with an exaggerated sigh of resignation. "It's not your fault."

"Mr. Ames is right. I heard stories about this guy, Miss Sydney. He isn't very nice."

Dramatically, Sydney sighed again. "Yeah, I know. Well, I suppose it's for the best." Out of the corner of her eye, she glanced at him, assessing his reaction to her sudden acceptance of defeat. "So, what should we do while we wait?"

"Do?" Claus looked stumped at the question.

"I know!" Sydney said. "Why don't we have a late lunch? Sure. That'll take our minds off things. Keep us from worrying about Jack."

"Lunch?" Claus said, brightening visibly.

"Yeah. Something really yummy. I think we deserve it, don't you?"

Claus nodded happily. "I could make a soufflé. I'm perfecting a new technique."

"A soufflé?" Sydney cried, trying not to think about how many seconds she was losing. "That sounds wonderful, and I'm starving. You'll never believe it, but I've been thinking about a soufflé all day. Are you sure you don't mind?"

"Mind?" Claus looked insulted. "I'm going to start right away. Gosh, Miss Sydney, you should have told me you were hungry."

"Well . . ." Sydney hung her head. "I didn't want to put you to all the trouble, and—"

"It's no trouble. I like cooking for you." Turning, Claus headed for the kitchen. "I'm going to make you the best soufflé you've ever tasted."

Breathlessly, Sydney waited until he'd disappeared into the kitchen. When she heard the refrigerator door open and the water in the sink turn on, she flew to the door, snatched her new white purse from the chair beside it, threw back the lock and was in the hall in a flash.

Down the corridor, the elevator doors were closed. Like a shot, she dashed toward them. Quickly, she pushed every down button on the panel, exhaling in relief as a door immediately opened to her call. Within seconds, she was tumbling out of the elevators and darting across the casino floor.

When she reached the front doors, panting and tugging at the tight skirt of her new summer suit, she scanned the row of limousines and taxis fretfully. No white limousine was in sight, and she was about to give up in frustration when, she saw a familiar head of thick black hair through the window of a taxi, just as it turned out of the driveway and onto the Strip.

"Quick!" Sydney screeched at the doorman. "Quick! I need a taxi."

The man gave her a bored look. "Yeah, yeah. Everyone needs one right this minute. You're just going to have to wait your turn, lady. All these cabs are already taken. If you want to wait inside, I can—"

Snapping open her purse, Sydney glanced at the bundles of hundred-dollar bills, all neatly bound with paper tape. She barely hesitated.

"Here," she cried, thrusting two bills at him. "I need a taxi *now!*"

The bell captain blinked at the money, then straightened his shoulders abruptly. "Yes, ma'am. Of course. Right away, ma'am," he said with clipped, polite respect. Raising his arm, he signaled to the nearest cab.

"For what it's worth, I heard it was his personal safe," Belinda said, smoothing back her disordered hair with one hand. Slumped in exhaustion in a deck chair, with a pink, bedraggled stuffed rabbit drooping from one hand, she shaded her eyes to check on the two children splashing and shouting happily in the pool with their nanny. "My guess is that it was an inside job."

"That's what I thought," Jack agreed. "I'm probably only one of a dozen names on his list. So far, he's just casting about at random."

In an ineffectual attempt to dry off, Jack pulled at the wet, grass-stained shirt plastered to his sides. The moment he'd appeared on the deck, two redheaded, wet little bodies had pounced on him, attaching themselves to his arms and soaking him to the skin.

After rolling back and forth in the grass with him for several minutes, they'd suddenly gotten bored and left him lying there on his back as they returned to the greater pleasures of the pool. Chuckling, Belinda had offered him a hand as he staggered to his feet and retrieved his suit jacket, shaken by the sheer force of their attack and wondering what it might be like to have one of those ruthlessly energetic little creatures of his own.

"Yes. But that doesn't mean Carlton's any less dangerous," Belinda replied. "You know, if it *is* an inside job, then I don't see how the girl can be involved. She's from out of town, you say?"

"Yes. From Venice Beach." Giving up on his shirt, Jack leaned back in his deck chair. "I believe her, Belinda. Call me a fool, but I believe her. Yes, she's holding something back from me, but I don't think it's about this business with Carlton. It could be something perfectly innocent. I just wish I knew *what* it was."

"I have to admit, the way you met her and her story about receiving someone else's letter sounds a little odd. And from what you've told me about her, she doesn't seem like the sort of woman to get involved with pornography." Belinda frowned, worried. "Yet you say you trust her."

"Absolutely. She's as honest as the day is long. I'd swear to it." Closing his eyes, Jack exhaled loudly and loosened his tie. "I just have this rotten feeling that everything's connected and that, somehow, Sydney's involved. Knowingly or not, she's at the center of this. I'm telling you, Belinda, that's what worries me."

For a few moments, his cousin studied him. "You've never been anxious about anything in your life," she said. "What you mean is, you're worried *for her.*"

Tentatively, Jack opened one eye but didn't reply.

Belinda's eyes widened. "You're in love with her," she exclaimed. "You've fallen in love with this woman, haven't you?"

Pushing against the arms of his chair, Jack sat up. "Look, I have a favor to ask you," he said, not answering her question. "Would you mind putting Sydney up for a few days? Just until I straighten all this out."

Astonishment colored Belinda's face. Then suddenly, she grinned. "Well, I'll be... I never would have believed it if I hadn't seen it with my own eyes. Imagine that. My wild cousin, Jack Ames, is finally in love. And Frenchie said you'd never fall. The family's going to go bananas."

Uncomfortable with Belinda's amusement, Jack glanced away. "Look, will you let her stay here until this blows over?"

"Of course she can stay here. I'm just flabbergasted, that's all. And happy for you. It's about time you took the big tumble."

"Well, keep it to yourself, would you?" Jack retorted. "I've got enough problems to handle right now. By the way, could I also borrow a car? If I try taking the limo from the hotel, Carlton's going to know my every move."

"Sure. Take the Rolls. The Jag's electrical system's acting up again, and the Mercedes is only a two-seater coupe."

"Thanks," Jack said, his voice dry. "But I don't think tooling around in a Rolls is going to contribute to my keeping a low profile. I'll take the Mercedes."

A quarter of an hour later, as Jack backed the little convertible coupe out of the garage and headed down the driveway, he saw Belinda hurrying toward him from the house. Pausing to wait for her, he fiddled with the controls and let the top down.

"You will be careful, won't you?" she asked anxiously, placing her hands on the window. "If Carlton seriously thinks you have his money, he isn't going to stop at much to get it back."

Jack gave her a quick, reassuring kiss on the cheek. "Don't worry, cousin. I can take care of myself. I've still got a few tricks up my sleeve. Which is something you, better than anyone, should know. After all, it was your husband who taught them to me, and we all know what a fighter Frenchie was."

Stepping back from the car, Belinda sighed. "Maybe," she said softly. "But then, Frenchie's not here anymore, is he? Tricks or no tricks."

Her words cut him to the quick. Only with an effort did he keep from flinching.

"I'll be fine," he said confidently. "I promise."

But when he slipped the car into gear and spun down the driveway, Jack couldn't suppress a bitter ache of self-reproach for having brought up Frenchie's name that way. Distressed, he wondered if Belinda would always be in mourning for her husband and if he, himself, would ever really accept the fact that his friend was gone.

So disturbed was Jack that, as he raced off toward the city, he didn't see the taxi parked discreetly beside the bushes across the street from Belinda's house or notice when it pulled slowly out and followed him through the quiet neighborhood.

# 9

$\longrightarrow \leftarrow$

"What in God's name do you think you're doing?" Rachel snapped. "I told you *never* to call me in my suite. Not for any reason."

They were sitting at the bar in the Jungle Nights Lounge, overlooking the Sunburst's main casino floor. Rachel swiped irritably at a bushy fern that threatened her perfectly styled hair. Then, as casually as possible, she raised her martini glass and took a sip, glancing around at the other customers.

"I think you're going to be glad," Tony said fawningly. "That woman, the one who was in room 203, remember? Well, I found her."

Rachel's head snapped up, satisfaction flashing in her cunning amber eyes. Hurriedly, she looked away. "Where?" she asked, pretending to watch an older couple across the bar.

"Believe it or not, she's downstairs now. At the roulette tables."

"My God," Rachel breathed, making the oath sound like a hiss. "We've got her."

"There's something else, though," Tony said nervously. "You told me to find her. To follow her. Well, I did. I found out where she's been. She's staying with Jack Ames. In his suite."

Rachel's eyes lit with surprise before she narrowed them and they became cool and calculating again. "Damn, that old snake is quick," she said with cool amusement, almost respect. "I thought it was a scream that Carl suspected Ames was involved. Now it looks like the old man wasn't so far off the mark, after all."

Tony twisted nervously on the stool beside her. "Well, it makes me nervous. What are we going to do, Rachael?"

Ignoring him, Rachael dipped her red-lacquered nails into her glass, picked out an olive and brought it to her lips. "So, Ames is involved with the woman," she said thoughtfully. She bit into the olive. "Interesting."

"But what are we going to do?" Tony repeated.

"I don't know. I have to think about this a minute. Ames doesn't concern me. Carlton's got Frank Bovo and his boys on that little problem." She risked a quick, vicious smile at Tony, then glanced away. "They'll take care of Jack Ames, all right. And more power to them. That guy always seems to be in the way. Ames isn't a problem for us. No, it's this woman that we've got to worry about. She's *our* business."

"I don't know," Tony fretted. "I don't like Ames being mixed up in this. I've heard some things about him, Rachel. He can be a mean customer when he wants."

"He's an imbecile," Rachel said with a sneer, thinking about the one time she'd met Ames and his eyes had flickered over her, dismissing her as easily as if she were an unsavory hors d'oeuvre. "A flashy, two-bit con man who's down on his luck."

"I still don't like it," Tony complained.

"Stop whining," Rachel said sharply. "I hate it when you whine. I already told you that Carlton's going to take care of him. There's nothing to worry about."

"But what'll we do about the woman?"

Rachel's smile was sly. "I think I know exactly what we should do. The simplest thing in the world. We wait. We wait for *her* to come to *us.*"

"Huh?"

"She has the key, Tony. Eventually, she'll try to use it. And when she does, you'll be waiting for her, won't you?"

Tony grinned. "Oh, I get it. Yeah. I'll be waiting for her."
Finishing off her drink, Rachel stood and collected her
purse. "Now show me who she is," she crooned as she
walked past Tony. "I want to see her damned face."

Miserable and dejected, Sydney leaned against the roulette table, an untasted gin and tonic at her elbow. Without
much interest, she watched the ball spin round and round,
finally settling on black 13. When the dealer raked up her
two five-dollar chips from the red 21 square, she barely noticed or even cared that she'd lost again.

Instead, the same scene kept replaying in her mind—Jack
pulling out of the driveway of that huge, luxurious house
and the beautiful blond woman traipsing lightly over the
immaculate lawn to bend close to him and receive his familiar, casual kiss.

Clutching the chip in her hand so hard that her knuckles
whitened, Sydney nearly moaned aloud.

"Bets, please," the dealer called.

Absently, she laid a handful of chips on the table, not
bothering to put them on any particular number. *It hurt,* she
wanted to cry out. It hurt so much she felt as if she were dy-
ing inside.

She knew she should go back upstairs. Jack was probably frantic with worry, to say nothing of Claus. But somehow, she just couldn't make herself go. Not yet. She
couldn't face him and ask the questions she knew she had to
ask. Not just yet.

As the ball began to spin around the wheel once more,
Sydney glanced up, wondering how in the world she could
ever confront Jack with what she'd seen, when suddenly she
became aware of a pair of eyes, as cold and metallic as gold
coins, staring at her from across the casino floor. Startled,
she met the woman's fierce gaze, strangely transfixed. If she
didn't know better, Sydney imagined fancifully, she'd almost believe that the woman hated her.

Cool as glass, perfectly groomed and sleek as a cat, the woman took a step in Sydney's direction, and Sydney felt an inexplicable tremor of fear course down her spine. The glint in the woman's eyes seemed menacing and viciously triumphant, she thought a little wildly.

Instinctively, Sydney felt the urge to flee, but as the woman took several more steps, she could only stare in fascinated, paralyzing dread.

When a hand suddenly seized her arm, Sydney jumped with fright. Terrified, she spun around and met Jack's glowering face.

"Just what the hell are you doing?" he demanded. "Do you realize that we've been looking everywhere for you? Claus is nearly out of his mind with worry. He thought Carlton grabbed you. He's been scouring the town searching for you. Yet here you sit, cool as you please, playing roulette as though you haven't a care in the world."

"Jack," Sydney gasped, weak with relief.

"Are these your chips?" he asked, scooping them up. "Come on. We're going upstairs, and don't give me any arguments. I've just about had it with you, Sydney. I swear to God, you'd try the patience of a saint."

"Jack," she said again. "That woman over there. She's been staring at me."

Jack raised his face. "What woman?"

Wheeling around, Sydney looked in the direction of the woman, but she had vanished. "She was right there. You aren't going to believe this, but I'd swear she was ready to attack me or something."

"Sure, Sydney," Jack muttered with barely concealed disbelief. "Sure she was. How many of those drinks have you had?"

"I haven't had anything to—" Sydney broke off, suddenly noticing the state of his clothing. His jacket was slung over his shoulder, his tie was askew and his shirtfront was rumpled and stained with grass. He looked anything but his normal, impeccably attired self. "My word, Jack. What happened to you? Are you all right? You're a mess. Did you have a run-in with those two thugs again?"

"No. With two five-year-olds," he said, leading her by the arm to the elevators. "Which was worse. They won hands down."

"Five-year-olds?" Reluctantly, Sydney let him steer her into an empty elevator, glancing over her shoulder in hopes of catching another glimpse of the strange woman. The woman was definitely gone.

When the elevator doors closed, Sydney snuck a quick peek at Jack's face. Impassively, he stared straight ahead in the manner of people in elevators everywhere. She wasn't sure what she expected his expression to be—guilty? secretive? dishonest?—but coolly enraged wasn't it. He certainly didn't look like a man who'd just stolen out to see another woman.

With a sinking heart, Sydney knew she had to ask. For her own sanity, she had to know the worst, once and for all.

"Jack," she said quietly, her voice thin with hurt. "Is there something you want to tell me?"

Glancing at her, he raised his eyebrows sardonically. "Me? I was wondering if there was something *you* wanted to say."

"Me? What would I have to tell you? I'm not the one who went sneaking off."

"Sneaking off?" His voice was incredulous. "What are you talking about? You were the one who gave Claus the slip and disappeared for three hours. *I* told you where I was going."

The elevator made a stop at the eighth floor, and the doors began to open.

"Did you? Did you really?" Sydney turned on him, her throat tight with the tears she refused to shed. "You said you were going to see a friend. You didn't mention she was blond and gorgeous and rich. Somehow, I guess, that part just sort of slipped your mind."

A short, squat man in a brown polyester suit that was several sizes too small for him started to step into the elevator. Jack raised a hand in warning.

"Take another elevator," he growled.

"Huh?" The man gaped at them. "But I'm going up."

"Take my advice, buddy. Wait for the next elevator." Jack scowled at Sydney. "Believe me, you don't want to get in this one."

With that, Jack punched the button, turning back to Sydney as the doors closed in the astonished man's face.

"You followed me," he accused. "My God, I can't believe it. You followed me."

"Of course I did. I thought you might get into trouble. I thought you might need me." Sydney choked back a sob. "I didn't know you were just going to see your lover."

"My lover? Oh, now that really takes the cake," Jack said, furious. "Belinda isn't my lover. She's my cousin. For God's sake, Sydney, are you a complete screwball?"

The elevator glided to a stop at their floor, but neither of them made a move to get out.

Confused, Sydney waved a hand vaguely. "Your cousin? She's your cousin?"

"Yes, she's my cousin. Has been my whole life. She and my aunt and uncle are my mother's only relatives. I went to see her kids and to ask her a favor. That's all."

As the full meaning of his words hit her, Sydney felt heat spread up her neck and across her face.

"Oh, wow," she groaned, too ashamed to look at him. "I feel really stupid."

"Yes, well, this probably hasn't been one of your best moments," Jack agreed. Suddenly, he smiled and shook his head with a short, bemused laugh. "You really are a nut sometimes. I mean, what were you thinking of? Did you forget that we'd just stayed up half the night making love? Weren't you listening when I told you that I was falling for you?"

Humiliated, Sydney squeezed her eyes shut. "Yes, I was listening. I just thought . . . I don't know. I just didn't think you meant it."

The elevator doors were jerking back and forth, unable to close with Jack's foot in the way. Taking her arm, he ushered her into the hall, then held her shoulders and turned her so that she was facing his wrinkled shirtfront.

"Why not?" he asked gently.

Sydney twisted uncomfortably under his hands, evading his eyes. "I don't know. I just didn't. And that woman—your cousin—she's so beautiful. I'm just not like her. I don't think I'm the sort of woman that men like you fall for."

Blank-faced, Jack stared at her. Abruptly, his eyes narrowed. Then he gripped her shoulders, spun her about-face and, without a word, marched her down the hall to the suite. He shoved open the door, then shut it behind them with a kick.

"Mr. Ames?" Claus rose to his feet and glanced at them warily.

"Go shopping, Claus," Jack commanded, propelling Sydney across the living room. "Go see a movie."

"But, Mr. Ames—"

"I said, *get lost*," Jack ordered.

"Yes, sir." He hesitated. "Hello, Miss Sydney."

"Oh, hello, Claus," Sydney called shakily over her shoulder as Jack rushed her into the bedroom and slammed the door.

In the bedroom, Jack led her toward the mirrored doors of the walk-in closet, jerking her to a halt before them.

"Look at yourself," he demanded. "Just one time, really look at yourself, Sydney."

Reluctantly, she raised her face, meeting the reflection of his eyes, black and intense and almost imploring. She looked very small standing in front of him, her head not quite reaching his chin, and his strong, tanned hands on her shoulders looked powerful and possessive.

"Not at me," he said. "Look at yourself. Take a good, long look."

Sheepishly, she glanced at the woman in the mirror. The woman who stared back could never be called slight nor even slender, yet the white linen suit with its scarlet braiding complemented her ample curves, making her appear shapely rather than frumpy. Her blue eyes were wide and bright and tilted mischievously at the corners. Even the blush that still burned shamefully on her own cheeks was merely a faint pink, becomingly flush on the woman in the mirror.

Surprised and deeply shaken, Sydney shrank from the reflection and glanced up tremulously at Jack.

The smile that spread across his face was slow and pleased. "Yes, you see, don't you? You've finally seen."

Sydney took an unconscious, lurching step forward. She lifted a hand and touched her fingers tentatively to the mirror as the woman there reached out to her.

Who was this? she wondered. The woman she was gazing at was pretty. How could she be this woman who looked so interesting and clever, so vivacious and playful, as though she was only waiting for something to make her laugh? Could she really be this woman—this woman who looked as if... as if she was in love?

From behind her, she heard Jack move. Pressing his body close to hers, he wrapped his arms around her waist and nodded at their figures in the mirror.

"And that," he said, his dark eyes shining, "that is the sort of woman a man like me falls for."

Tilting her head, Sydney looked again at her reflection. A bemused smile played on her lips. "You know," she murmured, "maybe I don't look half-bad."

Throwing back his head, Jack laughed delightedly, and in that second, Sydney recalled once more the image of the man and woman in the elevator outside the Starlight. How long ago was that? Days? Years?

In a rush, she remembered with stunning clarity her silent, hopeless envy, and suddenly she twisted in Jack's arms, burying her face in his grass-stained shirt and wrapping her arms tightly around him.

She *was* that woman in the mirror, she suddenly wanted to sing out. She was pretty and happy, and she was in love.

When Jack raised her chin with a finger and covered her mouth with his, she kissed him with all the joy and wonder swelling in her. Flattening her palms against his back, she let her hands absorb the warmth of his hard, smooth flesh even as her lips thirstily drank in his kisses.

When they stumbled to the bed, discarding clothing and kicking off shoes on their way, she went with him unhesitatingly, eagerly. And when they tumbled naked onto the sheets, she knew that this time she was giving him much more than her body. This time, she was giving him her heart.

"No way," Sydney protested just as Jack had known she would. Plumping up the pillow behind her, she flopped back and crossed her arms belligerently. "You're not stashing me away somewhere, Jack Ames. We're in this together."

"Sydney," Jack said patiently, still feeling lazy from their lovemaking and not in the mood for another knock-down-drag-out fight with her. "Be reasonable. Carlton doesn't fool around. He and his men play hardball. I don't think it's a situation you want to be involved in."

"Maybe not, but I'm in it till the finish. And that's that."

"All I'm asking is that you stay with Belinda for a few days."

"Forget it," she said. "I don't need a hideout, because I'm sticking with you. If you're so worried about this Carlton guy, then let's pack up and go stay somewhere else. We could stay at the Casbah."

"Why, of course, the Casbah," Jack said dryly. "Carlton will never think of looking for us there."

"Well, it was just a suggestion."

"Sydney, it doesn't matter where I go. If he wants to find me, he will." Reaching behind him, Jack took a cigarette from his gold case and lit it. "It's much better for me to be here in the thick of things. I can keep my eye on them. Discover what they're up to. And maybe, if I'm really lucky, I might even figure out who stole that money before I find myself taking a long, slow ride out into the desert with a couple of Carlton's business associates."

Sydney grimaced. "Ugh," she groaned. "Don't say stuff like that. You don't think he'd ever really do something like that, do you?"

"Considering that Carlton and I are close, loving pals who go back years?" He raised the cigarette to his lips. "Yes, I'd say he'd gladly plant me in the ground without blinking an eye, if he thought he'd get his two million back. The guy has a heart the size of a prune and just about as shriveled. I simply don't want you to be around if he gets impatient and starts dreaming up plots of revenge."

The expression in her eyes had grown worried, and she plucked absently at the sheet. "Then the thing we have to do is catch the real thief. Or thieves. You say you think it was someone close to Carlton?"

"Yes, that seems most likely. It could be a professional, but anyone who had the brains to pull a job like this wouldn't be stupid enough to steal from Carlton. It's got to be someone close to him. His manager, Bovo, maybe. That guy always struck me as greedy and dim-witted enough to do something like this."

"Yes, but is he still around? I mean, shouldn't we be looking for someone who's disappeared? If I'd stolen that much money, I don't think I'd show up for work the next day. I'd be on the next plane to the Far East."

Jack frowned at the glowing tip of his cigarette. "You have a point. Whoever pulled this job would want to be as far away as possible, as soon as possible. And yet, if someone close to Carlton had suddenly gone missing, I would have heard about it. Carlton would have heard about it...*and* already gone after him."

"So, maybe it's not someone close to him."

Jack's frown deepened. "Maybe."

Sliding down in the bed, Sydney rested her head on his chest. Jack reached for the ashtray and put out his cigarette.

"You know what?" she asked suddenly, lifting her head. "This sounds really crazy, especially when I think how much I hate the guy who's blackmailing...me. But if he hadn't, I would never have come to Vegas. And if I hadn't come to Vegas, I wouldn't have gotten that poor man's letter. And if I hadn't gotten the letter, I never would have gone to the Starlight and we never would have met."

Smiling faintly, only half listening, Jack stroked her hair.

"Pretty strange, huh?" she asked.

"Yes, very." Something was bothering him, gnawing away in the back of his mind, something he felt he should know.

"He's calling me tomorrow," she said. "Did I tell you?"

Jack barely heard her. So many things had happened, he wasn't sure which were connected with the theft. How could he put the pieces together when he didn't know which ones were important?

"Hmm?" he murmured. "What?"

"Oh, nothing. Never mind." Laying her head down again, Sydney traced a line through the black hairs on his chest.

"You know, there's something, Sydney," Jack said, his voice pensive. "Something I'm not seeing."

"Like what?"

Peering down his chin at her, he gave her a rueful look. "Don't get angry, but I can't help thinking that somehow you're the key to everything."

"Me? What could any of this have to do with me? I've never heard of these people before a few days ago." Tilting her head, she studied him. "Jack?"

Like the deep, shuddering reverberation of a gong, a memory stirred, and Jack felt his heart thud. The idea, so complete and so simple, came to him in a flash, and he knew. He knew. Not everything, but enough to feel sure he was right.

Then he shook his head.

"Jack?" Sydney said anxiously. "What is it?"

He gave a small, self-ridiculing smile. "No," he muttered to himself. "No, that can't be it. No one would be *that* stupid. Would they?"

"What? What are you mumbling about?" She was on her knees, gazing at him with concern. "What's wrong, Jack?"

"The key."

She gave him a blank look. "Key?"

Considering, he looked away. "Yes. The key. Maybe the answer's been staring us in the face the whole time.

"What are you talking about?"

"The key. The key that was with the letter. Remember? It wasn't *just* a letter. There was a key."

Sydney gaped at him.

"Maybe that's it, Sydney," he said excitedly, sitting up. "Maybe that's the answer. Think about it. The night after we met, your room was broken into. It was searched. What if someone was looking for that letter? For the key?"

"Holy Toledo," Sydney breathed.

"That's it. That's *got* to be it." Turning to her eagerly, he asked, "Where is the letter, Sydney? Where did you put it?"

In dismay, she stared at him. "You told me to throw it away."

Sitting on Jack's bed, Sydney dumped the contents of her old, bulky purse onto the sheet.

"Maybe I'm wrong. Maybe it's still in here somewhere," she muttered, pawing through the mess of old envelopes and gum wrappers. Tossing aside a paperback thriller, several tortured tubes of sunscreen, a spare pair of panty hose, three new rolls of black-and-white film and an extra waitressing apron, she sifted through the clutter.

"What's this?" Jack asked, picking out a small, four-bladed gadget.

She took it from him and tossed it in the pile along with a cassette that was spewing tape and a hastily rewrapped, half-eaten granola bar. "The insides of my blender. It conked out, and I've been meaning to get a new whatever that is."

"I can't believe you carry all this junk around with you. What do you need with a tube of toothpaste?"

With a glare, she took the tube from him, as well. "I might want to brush my teeth when I'm away from home." Seeing his look, she added defensively, "It's useful. All this stuff is useful."

"Uh-huh."

Flipping through a small date-book, the pages depressingly free of engagements, she suddenly cried, "I can't believe it! Jack! Here it is. Here it is."

Excitedly, she waved the smudged, crumpled envelope at him.

"Is the key there?" he asked.

Shaking the envelope, a huge grin spread over her face. "You betcha'. One small, mysterious gold key." Handing it to him, she leaned back with a smile, and watched him turn the key over in his fingers, examining it.

"C-53," he read, peering at the back. "Could mean anything."

"A safe-deposit box?"

"Maybe. Or a locker. An airport locker, a gym locker, anything. There's no real way of telling."

Snatching up a pencil and the dog-eared remains of a waitressing order pad from the pile she'd dumped onto the bed, he began to write furiously. Sydney watched him, her curiosity peaked.

Finally she ventured, "What are you writing?"

"A note to Carlton," he said, and flashed her a bright smile. "To buy us a little more time."

"What does it say?" she asked, trying to peer over his arm.

"It says," he told her, ripping off the check, "that I *might* know how to get back his money. And that I *might* be able to recover it for him *if* he agrees to leave us alone for twenty-four hours. It also says that he owes you $4.65 for a cheeseburger and a large diet cola."

"Very funny." Sydney scowled. "How are we ever going to make good on that? We don't have the slightest idea where Carlton's money is. How on earth are we going to find it?"

Folding the diner check, Jack caught her downcast look and gave her a roguish smile. "We get dressed, for starters. Then we go out into that bright and bustling city of sin called Las Vegas, Sydney, my darling, and begin the biggest treasure hunt of our lives."

Tripping along in high-heeled pumps down the wide concourse of McCarran Airport, struggling to keep up with Jack's long-legged stride, Sydney pulled at the sleeve of his jacket once more.

"But it's worth a try, isn't it?" she persisted. "We've checked the lockers in the hotel health spa—the men's *and* women's. We've checked the golf-course clubhouse, the train station, the three closest banks and two malls. You even had Claus sneak into the hotel employees' locker room."

"Sydney, I'm telling you, it's a waste of time." Jack pushed through the front door, then held it open for her. Dusk was beginning to settle over the desert, yet the air was still hot and heavy. Overhead, a jet rose into the sky, its engines roaring.

"I don't see how," she protested over the noise. "We can't think of anywhere else to look right now."

Signaling to an attendant to bring his car, he turned to her. In her simple, slim-fitting, sleeveless shift of rich China blue silk and the wide-brimmed white hat with its matching band, Jack thought she looked as fresh and delicate as the Spanish bluebells that dotted the hillsides of the island above his resort every spring. The urge to kiss her, to take her in his arms and slip that clingy silk dress off her body, was almost irresistible.

"I've got a better idea," he began suggestively. "What if we call it a night? We can start the search again in the morning."

Peering at him from under the brim of her hat, she read his meaning. "Oh no, you don't. We're going to find that money and get Carlton off your back. And I know exactly where we'll find it."

Opening the door of the little red convertible for her and stuffing a tip in the attendant's hand, Jack crossed to the driver's side.

"Sydney, the sort of person who would have access to Carlton's private safe probably doesn't frequent the bus station much."

Holding on to her hat as the car tore away from the curb, she shot him a look.

"Now, now," she censured as he raced the little car down the street, expertly dodging and weaving between cars. "Don't be snobby. Lots of people take buses. There's nothing wrong with them. Besides, we don't know exactly *who* took the money. We're only guessing."

With a rueful grin, Jack bowed his head. "I stand corrected. All right, if it's the bus station you want, we're on our way," he relented, letting his hand slip from the wheel and onto her leg as he darted around a truck and surged ahead.

"Good. I just hope you don't get us into an accident before we can find the place," she said, tugging at the hem of her dress and shoving away his hand. "Concentrate on your driving."

# 10

A musty, stale odor permeated the dingy waiting room of the bus station. With its dun-colored walls and rows of cheap plastic seats, the littered room of weary, indifferent travelers was dreary and cheerless.

Taking a fortifying breath, Sydney marched purposefully across the tile floor toward the bank of lockers against the far wall. Though she smiled back at Jack, she silently regretted her suggestion and had already begun to prepare herself for the inevitable letdown.

Jack was right, she admitted to herself. No one would hide two million dollars in a place like this. All she'd done was to lead them on another wild-goose chase.

"Well, here they are," she said, trying to sound enthusiastic. "The rows are divided by letters, at any rate."

Running his eyes down to the third row from the top, Jack nodded. "Yes, here are the Cs. We need C-53. Down there."

Sydney started down the row, her heels tapping against the tiles. "There's no 53," she said, though not with surprise. "It ends at 30."

"No, it doesn't. There are more around here." Jack had passed her and turned the corner of a small hallway leading to the rest rooms. "Sydney," he called, repressed excitement in his voice. "Here's C-53."

With a pounding heart, Sydney joined him in front of the locker. Anxiously, she watched Jack pull the key from his pocket. Glancing down at her, he grinned in anticipation.

With bated breath, she saw him fit the key to the lock and nearly shrieked aloud when it slid easily in.

Jack paused, his expression stunned. "My God," he said softly, then turned the key.

Crowding close to him, Sydney peered into the locker. A light blue, hard-sided suitcase sat alone in the tiny space, and when Jack lifted it out and set it on the floor beside them, she raised her hands to her mouth.

For a long moment, they gazed at each other, scarcely daring to believe their good luck. Jack's brilliant white smile was a little goofy with amazement.

"Open it," Sydney whispered. "Open it just a crack."

"I don't think you better do that," a strange voice said from the end of the narrow hall by the rest rooms.

Startled, Sydney wheeled toward the voice, just as a tall, blond man stepped from around the edge of the lockers. In his mid-twenties, he was more beautiful than handsome. His eyes, Sydney noticed at once, were strangely flat and vacant.

"Put your hands up where I can see them and step back," he ordered.

Beside her, Sydney felt Jack stiffen, as though poised to tackle the stranger. The man must have noticed, too, because he hesitated, almost recoiling. Then suddenly he smiled.

"I have a gun," he warned. "So step back."

Automatically, Sydney's eyes went to the bulge in the man's jacket pocket, and she gasped.

The skin around Jack's hard mouth had whitened in anger, and his eyes seemed to bore a hole through the man. "Tony Martin," Jack sneered. "So it was you. I should have guessed. I knew only an idiot would have pulled a stunt like this. Don't you know it's dangerous to steal from men like Carlton?"

With a nervous jerk of his head, the man's eyes flickered over them. "I said, put your hands up," he repeated, advancing. "I'll shoot if I have to. And it'll be the woman first."

A muscle in the side of Jack's face jumped, otherwise his expression of cool disdain didn't change. "Put your hands up, Sydney," he said softly. "It's all right."

"Step back, too," the man demanded.

"It's not going to do you any good," Jack said, the casual tone of his voice nearly masking the steely rage underneath. He shuffled his feet, moving only a few inches backward. "Take the money if you want. I'm sure Carlton will be interested to know you've got it."

Almost at the suitcase, Tony faltered. "He doesn't know. Carlton doesn't know a thing."

"Not yet," Jack said pleasantly. "But he will. Just as soon as we get back to the casino and tell him."

A glimmer of fear lit the man's eyes, then he gave a crooked grin. "You won't tell him. You wouldn't dare. He's already looking for you, Ames, and when he finds you, you're dead. You wouldn't have the guts to go to him."

"Try me," Jack snarled.

Before Sydney knew what was happening, Jack suddenly sprung forward. In a blur of color, she saw Jack's arm shoot out and the two men fall together.

"Run, Sydney," Jack shouted. He'd grabbed Tony's arm, and the hand that held the gun was raised above their heads.

Horrified, paralyzed with fear, Sydney stood rooted to the spot. Panting and cursing, clutched together in a deadly embrace, the two men struggled for the gun Tony held aloft. With his free arm, Jack struck the side of Tony's body.

"Sydney, run!" Jack bellowed again.

Terrified, Sydney drew back but didn't flee.

Once more, Jack slammed a fist into Tony's ribs, and the younger man grunted, releasing the gun so that it clattered to the floor. With a growl of rage, Jack threw him back into the lockers with such force that Tony groaned and slid to the floor, stunned.

Kicking away the gun, Jack went to snatch up the suitcase when he caught sight of Sydney staring at him, white-faced.

"I thought I told you to get out of here," he barked. "What are you doing?"

Stupefied, she could only gape.

He grasped the suitcase, grabbed her hand, then started at a trot down the hall, dragging her after him.

"Come on," he called. "Before he gathers his few wits together and comes after us."

"He had a gun. That man had a gun," Sydney babbled, grabbing at her hat as Jack flew through the bus station, tugging her behind him. "He was going to shoot us."

Kicking open the door, Jack hauled her down the sidewalk and into the parking lot.

"We could have been killed," she sputtered. "That man had a *real* gun."

Tossing the suitcase behind the seats, Jack sprang over the car door without bothering to open it and started the engine. "Get in, Sydney. For God's sake, get in the car."

Yanking at the door, she slid in beside him. She was still trying to shut the door as he pushed the accelerator and they squealed out of the parking lot in a shower of dust and gravel.

Wide-eyed, Sydney stared through the windshield as they swerved onto the street and roared past a group of startled pedestrians. Suddenly rousing herself, she twisted in her seat to look at the blue suitcase on the floor behind them. Cautiously, she leaned back and touched the metal clasp. When it clicked open easily, she stole a glance at Jack, who was watching her through the rearview mirror.

Almost fearfully, she cracked the lid of the suitcase. She peeked inside. Suddenly, with a loud gasp, she snapped it shut and threw herself back in her seat.

"What?" Jack cried. "What is it?"

"Oh, Jack." Raising her hands to her cheeks, Sydney panted. "It's there. The money's there. Lots of it. Lots and lots of it."

"Y-y-y-e-e-s-s!" Jack hollered at the top of his lungs, gripping the steering wheel tightly in excitement. His smile was wide and elated. "We've got them, Sydney. We've got them now!"

"I can't believe this. I can't. Just think of it. In the last few days, I've been blackmailed, vandalized, terrorized and now almost killed." Beaming, she turned to him. "Oh, Jack. I've never had so much fun in my whole life."

For a long time, Sydney stood before the full-length mirror in the enormous marble-tiled bathroom. She knew she was stalling, putting off the moment when she would have to open the door and join Jack. Yet still she hesitated, and the hand she raised to brush through her loose hair was trembling.

It was crazy, she told herself for the hundredth time. Jack's scheme was crazy, terrifying and more than a little dangerous. Yet...

Once more, the thrill of excitement coursed through her. If they could pull it off, if they could walk in there and do what he assured her they could do, it would be the most daring and lucrative con Las Vegas had ever seen.

And she would have been in on it.

Staring in the mirror, Sydney scrutinized her appearance. The long, cherry-red sequined gown, held up only by two thin satin straps, made her look elegant and wealthy—just the look, Jack insisted, she would need. But with her blue eyes overly large and bright and her color high with anticipation, she seemed more like a woman on the verge of nervous collapse.

When she was a child, her favorite ride at the fair had been the roller coaster. The feeling she had now was very much like the one she'd experienced all those years ago. Then, fear and dread had made a knot in her stomach, and as much as she'd always wanted to get off the ride before it was too late, she knew—just as she did now—that she would not. The allure was too great. This, she thought, was what Jack had meant about the thrill of "pulling a job," and he was right. It was heady stuff.

With a heart that raced a little too fast, Sydney studied her reflection thoughtfully. How much she'd changed in just a few short days. She was no longer Syd the shy frump, no longer Sydney the unwilling actress. Instead, she'd become this woman she saw before her now, stylish, adventurous, and... and yes, attractive. The change was almost too radical to contemplate.

It occurred to her that, if it hadn't been for Jack, she might never have known she could be this woman, and that thought brought with it a whole host of unwelcome fears. Could she continue to be this woman when she was back at Venice Beach? Because, she knew, the day when they would part was growing nearer all the time. She would return to her world, and Jack, well, he would return to that island in the Bahamas—so distant, so far-removed from her.

It was, she told herself, the way things had to be.

Swallowing hard, Sydney stepped back from the mirror, running a hand down the clinging dress to smooth it. The idea of leaving Jack, of never seeing him again, was too heartrending to think about. Not now, she told herself. She wouldn't think about that now. Tomorrow, when there would be no avoiding it, was soon enough.

Tonight, she was going on a roller-coaster ride with him, and no matter what the danger, she was going to savor every moment. With that decision made, Sydney resolutely turned, and headed out to the living room where Jack waited.

Handsome and debonair in his black tuxedo, the sight of him nearly made her rush forward and throw her arms around him. Instead, she strolled calmly across the thick carpeting and paused in front of him.

His eyes shone, and his smile was elated, whether from anticipation of the game they were about to play or from the sight of her, she couldn't be sure. When he backed up a step to better take her in, then gave a silent whistle, she got her answer—and a swell of pleasure.

"Sydney, you are truly, absolutely stunning. You take my breath away."

She felt her face grow a shade warmer. "I'll do, I guess," she said modestly, then gave him a grin. "I mean, for a woman about to have a nervous breakdown."

Draping an arm around her shoulders, Jack pulled her close and kissed her forehead softly.

"We don't have to do this," he said. "We could put the money back now, and no one would ever be the wiser. I admit, I wouldn't mind having a little fun at Carlton's expense. He certainly deserves it. Tony Martin, too. But it's not worth it, not if you don't want to go through with this."

Sydney barely hesitated. "No, it's worth it. I want to do this. I just wish we could see Tony Martin and Carlton's faces when they realize what we've done."

"You just may have the opportunity." Jack squeezed her shoulders. "You've got spunk, Sydney. I knew it the first time I laid eyes on you. By the end of the night, we'll have given those two a memorable dose of their own medicine."

From the hallway, Claus cleared his throat. "It's all set up, Mr. Ames. You were right. They didn't recognize her name at the cashier's office."

A slow, devilish smile began to grow on Jack's lips. "Wonderful. Then the game is on." Slipping Sydney's arm through his, he said, "Miss Sydney Stone of Venice Beach, California, you now have a credit line at the Sunburst Casino and Hotel of two million dollars. Do you have anything to say for yourself?"

With a nervous smile, Sydney let him lead her to the door. "Just one thing. You'd better not forget to tell me what to bet on."

\* \* \*

"Mr. Ames," the doorman said, taken back. "We didn't . . . didn't expect you this evening."

"I'll just bet you didn't, Walter," Jack said amicably enough, although his eyes glittered briefly. "Is Mr. Van Hausen here tonight?"

"Mr. Van Hausen?" Walter asked as though he'd never heard the name before. Nervously, he glanced behind him. "I mean, no, sir. Not yet."

"Good. You remember Miss Sydney Stone, don't you, Walter?"

It was obvious to Jack that the man recognized the name, certainly having been warned of an unknown high roller who'd suddenly made a surprise appearance at the casino less than an hour earlier.

"Yes, of course. Miss Stone." The man nearly bowed in his confusion.

"I've promised to teach Miss Stone a bit about gambling tonight." Strolling to the doors to the private casino, Jack added over his shoulder, "Make sure we're comfortable, Walter. We wouldn't want Miss Stone to dislike the games, would we?"

Looking bewildered and alarmed, Walter stared after them. Just as the doors were opened for them, Jack saw the man suddenly dash away, most likely to the nearest phone with a direct line to Carlton's private office.

A frosty smile touched Jack's mouth, and he took Sydney's arm and led her into the casino. The minute Carlton heard the news, he would begin to suspect, Jack knew. But of course, by then it would be too late.

Nodding and murmuring greetings to familiar faces around the room, Jack steered Sydney toward the baccarat tables. Jack felt a swell of pride at walking beside her, elegant in her sparkling ruby-colored gown, as well as a warm rush of delight for her as the crowds around the tables turned to stare, making way for them.

In a room filled to overflowing with wealthy women, painstakingly groomed and draped heavily in jewels, he thought Sydney stood out like a brilliant, newly blossomed rose. No makeup was necessary to enhance her fair, flawless complexion, and although she was wearing not a single jewel, she outshone every woman she came near.

Once more, Jack came close to blurting out the question he'd been holding back all day. Ever since he'd spoken with Belinda and she had guessed his feelings for Sydney, he knew what he intended to do. He had fallen in love with Sydney, he told himself again with a thrill of wonder. After all the years of casual affairs and living alone, she had walked into his life, knocking him off his feet, creeping into his heart and sending his soul soaring to new heights.

He imagined again how he would tell her his feelings and ask her to come with him. Once more, he pictured the look she would have the first time she saw his little island paradise and the joy he would feel the first time he lay with her on his bed in the cool, high-ceilinged room overlooking the Atlantic.

Life had never seemed so wonderful before, and he knew it was because suddenly the future he envisioned was one filled with love and companionship—because his life would be shared with Sydney.

When Sydney poked him in the ribs with her elbow a second time, Jack finally came back to earth. She was peering at him with a puzzled look, and he gave her a happy, distracted smile.

"Jack," she said under her breath. "Wake up, would you? What am I supposed to do?"

"Do?" He was watching her mouth, enjoying the way her full, soft pink lips formed each word.

"Gambling?" she whispered urgently. "Remember? You're supposed to show me how?"

Jack cleared his throat. "Oh, yes. Gambling."

"Well?"

"Okay. Well, this is baccarat." Nodding at the kidney-shaped baccarat table before them, he explained the game as simply as possible. "The rules are fairly uncomplicated. Each player takes a turn at being what is called the bank. Unlike blackjack, in which every player at the table gets cards, the person who is the banker deals out only two sets of cards—two cards to what's termed the player and two to the bank, for a total of only four cards. He or she deals from a plastic cardholder called a shoe. The other players around the table bet on which of these two hands, the bank or the player, will get closer to nine. A third card can be dealt to either the player or the bank after the first two cards are turned faceup."

She nodded, a tiny crease of concentration between her eyebrows. "That sounds simple enough."

"It is. The exciting part is that either hand can win with practically any number. Tens and face cards count as zero, so if the banker's hand goes over nine, the player's hand could win with just one."

"All right. I think I understand. But how will I know whether to bet on the banker or the player?"

Jack gave her a confident, slightly wicked smile. "I'll tell you. You see, I've got a method. It's easy, really. With enough practice."

"Practice?"

"At playing the odds."

Sydney stared at him. "Playing the odds is not fool-proof. You know it's not. It would take a computer to figure out the odds with any certainty."

"Trust me, Sydney."

Unhappily, Sydney ran the tip of her tongue over her bottom lip. "Oh, boy. I can't believe we're really going to do this."

"It'll be fun. A piece of cake. Don't worry."

"Will you tell me how much to bet?"

Jack's smile suddenly grew more rakish. "Now, that's the very best part of baccarat. You see, it's the one game in the house in which hundred-thousand-dollar bets are common-place and million-dollar bets not unusual. In other words, the sky's the limit."

"But what if I lose?" she asked, her voice a little panicked. "If we bet that much money and lose, we'll be in *real* trouble. You said we were only going to borrow Carlton's money. We've got to give the two million back."

"We'll give it back—after we win a small fortune from Carlton with his own cash. Don't worry, we aren't going to lose. I *never* lose. I have a secret method, Sydney. You're just going to have to believe me."

Nervously, she wet her lips with the tip of her tongue. "A secret method?"

"Yes. Secret."

"What is it?"

Jack smiled and shook his head silently.

Sydney gazed at him. "Well, couldn't we still start out with something a little less risky? Those bets are so high, Jack. Couldn't we play roulette for a while?"

"All right, we can begin with roulette if you want. But Sydney," Jack said earnestly, "don't forget that the only way to win big is to play big. If I've learned anything, it's that you have to take the chances as they come. When it comes right down to it, most of life is just one, big, high-stakes gamble."

"Yes," she said cryptically. "I'm beginning to figure that out."

If she imagined she'd already had more fun in her life than she'd ever had before, Sydney thought, her cheeks flushed with excitement, it was because she didn't know what Jack had planned for her. Sitting at a roulette table, dropping handfuls of thousand-dollar chips on the numbers he suggested—as well as a few she herself felt were promising—she watched in amazement as the stacks of chips before her grew and grew until they covered the whole corner of her space at the table.

"Let it ride," Jack whispered from close behind her. Beaming, she nodded, letting the winnings from her last bet rest on the black 21 square. When the tiny ball began to rotate round and round the wheel, she gripped Jack's hand, her heart pounding.

The ball clattered to a stop on the wheel at black 21.

"All right!" Sydney shouted, bouncing up and down on her stool, then twisting backward to throw her arms around Jack. "We did it! Isn't it wonderful?"

The expression on Jack's face was one of pure happiness. With glowing eyes, he returned her embrace, kissing the top of her head.

"*You're* wonderful," he murmured, his voice so quiet that only she could hear. "How about some champagne?"

"I thought you said we shouldn't—"

"I changed my mind." Raising his hand to signal a waiter, he kept his hand on her bare shoulder, his strong fingers caressing her neck. "Don't want to be *too* serious, you know."

From the roulette wheels, they moved to the crap table, and there again they couldn't seem to lose. Shaking the dice in the cup, Sydney threw them down the table again and again, cheering and clapping her hands each time they won.

It was the most exciting evening she'd ever spent. Sipping champagne, pausing to catch their breath on the terrace outside the casino and to nibble the savory hors d'oeuvres provided by the hotel, dancing with Jack in the center of the private casino after a particularly stunning win, she felt like the heroine of a new and more exciting version of *Cinderella*.

Out on the terrace again later in the evening—taking a short break to calm down after a tense bout with roulette and to allow the casino to gather up, count and credit her winnings—Sydney felt Jack stiffen beside her.

"What is it?" she asked. "What's wrong?"

Jack's eyes were focused, steely and suddenly serious, on the casino floor, visible through the doors.

Very softly, he said, "He's here."

Sydney whirled. "He is? Where?"

Without altering his gaze, Jack gave a tiny toss of his head to indicate the man. "There. The gray-haired man next to the woman in black."

"Where? Oh, yes. So that's the guy who—" Sydney clutched Jack's arm. "Jack. Jack, that's her. That's her. The woman in the casino downstairs. Remember I told you she looked like she wanted to scratch out my eyes? That's her."

"My God," Jack breathed. "Of course. Rachel."

"Jack!" Sydney whispered fiercely, clutching Jack's arm. "I think the man from the bus station, Tony Martin, was in the casino, too. In fact, I'm sure he was there."

"Yes, I see," Jack murmured, a cool smile forming on his lips. "I finally see."

"See what?" Sydney said, shivering at the sight of the beautiful brunette. "What do you see?"

"I couldn't figure out how Tony could have stolen the money from Carlton on his own. He isn't bright enough. And now, I know. That woman, Sydney, is Rachel Bennet. At any rate, that's what she calls herself. You'd be hard-pressed to find a meaner, nastier bit of goods than Rachel in all of Las Vegas. She's Carlton's mistress. Has been for the past few years."

"I don't understand. What does she have to do with Tony?"

"I'll bet you anything she's the brains behind the theft. Tony is just her dogsbody. Maybe they're lovers. It's Rachel who would know the combination to Carlton's safe. She would know when he was out of town. My God, that woman *was* after you, Sydney. She must have known who you were and that you had the key to that locker."

"Do you think she was the one who had my room vandalized?"

"Not vandalized. Searched. And yes, I do. I'll bet you anything, she and Tony were looking for that key."

With a wave of resentment, Sydney stared at Rachel Bennet. "She's the one who went through all my stuff. The one who scared me half to death."

"Which was probably a large part of her purpose," Jack said grimly. "Yes, I think you're right. She was the one who gave the orders, all right. But don't worry, Sydney. I think you're about to make up for your losses."

Sydney couldn't resist a small smile. "I am?"

"Yes, you are. In fact, I think it might be time for a little baccarat. What do you say?"

Sydney took his arm. "I think that sounds like a wonderful idea."

In the center of a group of wealthy gamblers and guests of the casino, Carlton Van Hausen and Rachel Bennet stood chatting. Yet, as Sydney and Jack strolled leisurely past the group, their conversation trickled off and slowly died. Unable to resist a backward glance, Sydney saw them watching her and Jack—Rachel's eyes glinting like gold daggers and Carlton's cold as steel.

Jack patted her arm. "Don't worry," he said soothingly. "We're going to play a few more quick hands. Then we'll be gone before they know what hit them. Do you remember what I told you about baccarat?"

Finding an open seat at one of the tables, Sydney nervously clutched the edge of her stool. Because of the size of the wagers at this table, no chips were visible. All bets were recorded by computer.

When Jack directed her to bet ten thousand dollars on the banker's hand at the start of the next new game, Sydney obeyed, her heart in her throat. With her eyes riveted to the deck and to the four cards that lay facedown on the table, she waited anxiously for them to be turned up. The banker won with a six, and Sydney let out a sigh of relief.

"A hundred thousand dollars," Jack whispered into her ear. "On the banker again."

"How much?" she whispered back.

"You heard me."

When once more the banker won with a nine, her relief was almost dizzying.

"One million," Jack said softly beside her ear. "On the banker."

Wheeling in her seat to stare at him, Sydney felt her mouth go dry. "Jack—"

"Go on. Remember what I said about winning big. And don't forget that I've got my little secret."

"Yes, but—"

"Go on, Sydney, my love."

Startled at his use of the endearment, she could barely articulate the amount when her turn came to lay her bet. In a frightened squeak, she declared, "One million dollars. On the banker."

Almost as an afterthought, she added weakly, "Please."

## 11

------ ◆ ------

At Sydney's words, a hush fell instantly over the other players at the table. Deadpan, the dealer merely blinked at her, but she saw tiny beads of perspiration spring out on his upper lip as he repeated her bet to the supervisor standing behind him.

A crowd had begun to gather, drawn instinctively to the tension like bees to honey. They jostled and peered over one another's shoulders as the player who was elected to deal pulled out first one card, then another with a shaking hand.

Facedown, the cards lay on the green baize table. A breathless silence had descended over the crowd, and still the cards lay facedown, as though the dealer and the player couldn't bring themselves to turn them up.

Dry-mouthed and cold with fear, Sydney watched as the cards were slowly turned, one at a time. Her palms were sweaty, and she clenched her hands tightly together in her lap, scarcely aware her lips were moving in a silent plea.

"Nine beats eight," the dealer called. Without glancing up, he continued, "The bank wins."

A silent rustling, an almost universal sigh, rippled through the crowd. Faint, too stunned to fully comprehend his words, Sydney continued to stare at the cards.

"Congratulations," Jack said quietly in her ear, as cool as if she'd just been awarded a free box of cornflakes at the supermarket. "You've just won eight million dollars."

It was lucky for her that he already had a strong, steady hand on her shoulder. When her stool toppled over, he grabbed her, lightly setting her on her feet.

"Jack," she said, her voice hollow and faint. "I think I'm going to be sick."

His arm went protectively around her, and he landed a kiss on her forehead. "Here, have a sip of champagne."

Waving the glass away, she drew back into his arms. "No, Jack," she breathed. "Look."

Glancing in the direction of her gaze, he merely paused, then smiled icily at a steel-eyed Carlton and an ashen-faced Rachel Bennet. Helping her around the table, making their way through the congratulatory crowd, Jack paused several feet from the couple.

"Carlton," Jack acknowledged easily, bowing his head slightly.

"Jack." The single word was laden with such menace that Sydney nearly cowered.

"I really enjoyed myself tonight," Jack said breezily. "Had a terrific time. Sorry we can't stay longer, actually."

"I'm sure," Carlton said acidly.

"Wonderful about first-time luck, isn't it?" He squeezed Sydney's shoulders chummily. "She was great."

"I want to talk with you, Jack. I got your note."

"Sure, Carl. Sounds great. Let's do lunch tomorrow." He turned as though to go, then halted and looked back pointedly at Rachel. "You should keep your eye on her, Carlton. Rachel's looking a bit peaked. Thanks again. For everything."

Out in the hall, Sydney sagged against Jack's arm. "Lunch?" she exclaimed. "You're going to *do lunch?*"

Jack chuckled. "Not if I can help it. In fact, Claus is at Belinda's with all our luggage this very moment, if I'm not mistaken. I didn't think it would be a good idea to go back to the suite."

Sydney frowned. "But what about our money? How will we get the money?"

Jack started down the hall toward the elevators. "Carlton may be a greedy, coldhearted bastard, but he's a businessman through and through. He has no proof, Sydney. Only suspicions. The only two people who know what we've done are Rachel and Tony. And I think it's a pretty safe bet that they aren't going to say anything."

"So we're just going to walk up to the cashier's office and ask for our eight million dollars?" Wide-eyed, Sydney followed him into an elevator.

"Actually, it's $9.7 million dollars. You were on a pretty fair roll earlier, you know."

Realization of the enormity of what they had done, the mind-boggling consequences of that one winning hand, suddenly hit Sydney anew and she slumped against the elevator wall.

"Pinch me, Jack. I think I must be dreaming."

His laugh was low and jubilant. "You're not dreaming, Sydney. But we're not done yet."

"We're not?"

"Did you forget? We've got to give the two million back."

Sydney groaned. Then suddenly she straightened and gave him a close, suspicious stare. "How?" she asked. "Just how did you manage to do it? How did you know? I mean, it seemed as though you knew each and every card that was going to be played."

"Did it really?" He looked pleased.

In horror, Sydney gaped at him. "You mean, you *didn't* know?"

"Well, not exactly. No."

Weakly, Sydney leaned against the elevator. "Are you telling me you guessed? You *guessed?* What about everything you said about never losing?"

Jack raised his eyebrows and shrugged. "Well, it was a fifty-fifty chance, wasn't it?"

"I don't believe this. All that stuff about a secret method and years of practice and I should trust you because you know what you're doing—and in the end, all you were doing was *guessing*." Sydney began to feel a little ill again. "Was it really just luck? Just plain, dumb, blind, old luck?"

Jack beamed as though she'd said something brilliant. "Precisely."

"Oh, my God." She put an unsteady hand to her cheek. "And all along I believed you. I actually believed in your 'secret' method."

Jack frowned. "But that *is* the secret," he began as the elevator doors opened on the casino. "And that's why I couldn't tell you. You had to see it work, yourself, in order to believe in it."

Sydney stared at him in bewilderment.

"Sometimes, Sydney," he said with unusual intensity, "you just have to close your eyes and rely on fate. Because—if you have the strength to trust in luck—you can never truly lose. The only sure way of losing is to do nothing at all."

Skeptically, she scowled at him. "Luck? That's what you relied on tonight?"

"Of course." Helping her from the elevator, he stopped her just outside and ran a finger tenderly down her cheek. "You see, Sydney, I've been on a run of good luck lately. Ever since the day I met you. And that *is* something I believe in."

It was daylight when Sydney finally rolled over sleepily, yawning and stretching. The first thing she became aware of was that she was still wearing the red-sequined dress. The rest came flooding back in a rush that made her sit bolt upright in bed.

Had they really done that last night? Had they really bet one million dollars of Carlton's money at one of Carlton's own baccarat tables . . . and *won?*

Beside her, Jack was still deep in sleep, his face pressed into his pillow. He'd gotten as far as undoing his tie and loosening the top studs of his evening shirt before falling onto the bed beside her and slipping almost instantly into an exhausted sleep.

It had been nearly dawn before they finally wheeled into the driveway of Belinda's low, rambling house. On the nightstand beside her, Sydney glanced at the innocuous brown envelope that Belinda would deliver to the front desk of the Sunburst this afternoon. With a thousand-dollar chip Sydney had discovered in the bottom of her evening bag, a small, gold-plated key and a bus ticket to Cincinnati, Jack felt certain that Carlton would understand when he received the envelope.

Smiling faintly, she remembered how she had laughed last night when Jack had packed exactly two million dollars into the blue suitcase, then added a single dollar bill as a joke—"interest," he had called it, on a generous loan.

Across the room on a chair sat two steel, double-locked cases containing over four million dollars apiece. Once again, Sydney closed her eyes and inhaled slowly to steady herself.

No, she decided. It hadn't been a dream. Unbelievable, unthinkable even, but not a dream.

Stealthily, careful not to wake Jack, Sydney slipped from the bed and padded across the room to the door. In the early-morning light, she wanted more than anything to quietly sip a cup of coffee in an attempt to come to terms with the stunning events of last night.

For starters—she finally allowed herself to consider the prospect—she was rich. *Rich.* It had a funny sound, that word. What in the world, she thought as she turned the corner to the kitchen, was she ever going to do with so much money?

As she stumbled sleepily into the kitchen, Claus turned from the kitchen sink, and Sydney pulled up short.

"Claus. What are you doing up?"

"It's eleven o'clock, Miss Sydney. Do you want brunch?"

With a silent sigh, Sydney shook her head, relinquishing any hope of solitude. "Just coffee. Black and strong. I think I had too much champagne last night."

Wordlessly, Claus turned to pour her a cup from the pot on the counter. For the first time, Sydney realized that the big man was avoiding her eyes.

"Here," he said nicely enough as he set a cup on the table before her, but still he wouldn't meet her gaze.

"Claus, is something wrong? Are you upset about something?"

Uncomfortably, he stood at the sink, his huge hands hanging at his sides. Yes, she thought, there was something definitely troubling him.

"Claus?" she urged gently.

Glancing at her, he dug into the pocket of his white jacket, produced a crumpled piece of paper and handed it to her.

"This man called for you last night, Miss Sydney. The hotel forwarded the call to Mr. Ames's suite."

She didn't need to read the note to know what it was about. Swallowing, Sydney set down her cup, spread out the note with the flat of her hand and read. Just seeing the words made her heart grow cold and her throat tighten.

Noon, he said. He wanted to meet her at noon in a motel called the Desert Arms.

Crumpling the paper in her fist, she took a deep, ragged breath. Then she remembered what time Claus had said it was. Eleven. But that meant noon was only an hour away!

Springing to her feet, Sydney turned to fly from the room, when she saw the bald, unhappy giant studying her from beside the kitchen sink.

"Don't ask me, Claus. There's no time to explain."

"Miss Sydney," he grumbled, his broad face creased with concern.

"Please, Claus."

"If you're going to meet this person, you should tell Mr. Ames. I don't know what that note means, but I know you should tell him."

"No!" Sydney exclaimed in a panic, then quickly got herself under control again. "No, Claus. Jack is sleeping. I don't want to bother him. Do you understand? I don't want him to be bothered with this."

Claus made no reply.

"Promise me. Promise me you won't tell him," Sydney pleaded.

"I can't, Miss Sydney. I can't do that. If you're in trouble—"

"I'm not in trouble. It's just that this is . . . private. It has nothing to do with Jack."

Claus's face was glum.

"Please. Please promise me you won't say anything to Jack."

Unhappily, reluctantly, he slowly nodded.

"Thank you, Claus. Oh, thank you," Sydney cried as she flew from the kitchen to the phone in the living room, already calculating how long it would be before a taxi could come to fetch her.

Fifteen minutes later, seated morosely at the kitchen table, Claus heard the front door shut behind Miss Sydney. With worried eyes, he gnawed absently on his thumb.

He shouldn't have promised, he thought again. He should never have promised not to say anything. But he *had* promised, and now there was nothing he could do about it.

Heavyhearted, he sat like a bull at the gates of the ring, straining to rush forward, then backing up with sudden foreboding. He knew he should wake Mr. Ames. Yet he'd promised Miss Sydney.

In a muddle, he stared at the kitchen table. It was several minutes before his eyes focused on the screwed-up piece of notepaper. Reaching for it, he smoothed it out, mouthing the words silently to himself as he read.

The idea formed slowly in his mind, but when it finally came to him, it was as though a huge and crushing weight had been lifted from his shoulders.

He had promised Miss Sydney not to *say* anything, and he wouldn't. But he'd never promised not to show Mr. Ames the note. Vaguely, Claus knew the distinction was a little fine, but once he'd seized on the idea, relief carried him out of the kitchen on a relentless course.

Despite her panic and the wild rush with which she'd left Belinda's house, Sydney arrived at the Desert Arms motel fifteen minutes early. Located in the seedier downtown section of the Strip, the motel was run-down and depressingly shabby. From across the street, she stood and regarded the building with dread.

The motel parking lot was nearly empty, and a newspaper blew forlornly across the weed-choked pavement. Once more, Sydney glanced at her wristwatch, not wanting to cross the street and find the room even a minute before she absolutely had to.

At ten to twelve, a yellow, rusting compact car with a battered front fender pulled into the lot and a thin, dark-haired man in jeans and a tight black turtleneck got out and entered the third ground-floor room on the right.

Sydney's heart began to pound. Reluctantly, she started across the street.

Jack gripped the wheel of the sleek, black Rolls, taking a corner at fifty so that beside him Claus braced himself against the door and Belinda was bounced around in the back seat. Cold fingers of fear grasped at his spine, and his face was grim with anger.

When Claus had first shaken him awake, he hadn't believed it. His first reaction, before the icy terror gripped him, was fury that Claus could have let her go. But one look at the misery in the man's eyes had made him grit his teeth and swallow the worst of his anger.

"What time is it?" he asked now, his voice harsh with anxiety.

"Five to twelve," Belinda answered. Leaning forward, she peered over the seat. "She'll be all right, Jack. He'll never hurt her, I'm sure of it. Whatever else blackmail is, it isn't a crime of violence."

Wordlessly, Jack met Claus's eyes in silent agreement. "It is now," he said ominously. "It is now."

His name, he said, was Jimmy Bird. Perhaps because she was so terrified, the name struck her as funny and Sydney nearly began to laugh. With an effort, she swallowed the hysterical giggles.

"You have the money?" he asked. Tall and bony, with lank dark hair, a beaklike nose and bad skin, he reminded Sydney of a cartoon vulture she'd seen on television. Nervously, his eyes flickered around the room, and she began to realize that he was at least as frightened as she.

The thought did little to comfort her. Somehow, she understood intuitively that a person like Jimmy Bird was most dangerous when he was spooked.

"Yes. I have it. Fifteen thousand dollars. Just like you said." Her throat was painfully dry, and although she swallowed several times, it stayed dry. "Do you have the . . . the pictures?"

Slyly, ferretlike, he cast her a glittering, bright-eyed glance. Was he on drugs? Sydney suddenly wondered as the fear rose in her until it seemed an almost physical pain.

"I've got them, but I want another five thousand."

"Another five thousand? But you already raised the price—"

Flicking back the curtains and peering into the parking lot, then stepping back into the center of the room, he sneered at her. "If you don't want to pay me, there are others who will. This is your last chance. You've stalled too long already.''

Clutching her purse to her chest, Sydney inhaled roughly. ''All right. I'll give you twenty thousand. But if you *ever* bother my sister again, I swear to you I'll go to the police myself.''

His smile was oily. ''Don't give me that line, lady. We both know your fancy sister ain't ever going to want anyone to know about these babies.'' From the back pocket of his jeans, he pulled out a thin manila envelope, folded down the center, and tapped it against the palm of his hand. ''Let's see the money.''

''The pictures first.''

His sallow-skinned face flushed red with anger, but he threw the envelope on the bed. ''Help yourself.''

Cautiously, afraid to take her eyes off him, Sydney reached for the envelope, picked it up and undid the clasp. Although she'd known about them for weeks she felt tears well in her eyes when she actually saw the pictures.

There were seven or eight of them, and though they were definitely pornographic, they could have been worse, she tried to tell herself. At least Sheila was wearing a minimum of lingerie in most of them. Still, the thought of her sister putting herself through such a humiliating ordeal was heartbreaking.

When she glanced up from the pictures, catching Jimmy Bird's lurid, cunning smile, hot anger rose in her, burning through her veins, and she gave him her haughtiest, coldest look of disdain. She wanted to call him names, to tell him what she thought of him. But of course, she knew, he wouldn't care. Anyone who would stoop to blackmail was past caring what anyone thought about him.

''Here's your money.'' She nearly spat the words as she opened her purse and tossed four bundles of bills onto the grimy bedspread. ''If I were a man, I'd stuff it down your throat.''

"Now, that would be a waste of good cash, wouldn't it?" she heard as the door flew open.

Together, she and Jimmy Bird spun and stared at Jack, who stood glowering in the doorway.

Stepping into the room with a cold smile on his lips, he continued, "Especially when you can use one of these."

Before Sydney could blink, Jack had raised a fist and landed it squarely in Jimmy Bird's face, knocking him backward and onto the bed. Jack gave a small flinch, raising his fist and shaking it. Then he advanced on the cowering man, who sprawled across the bed, tentatively touching his fingers to his bloody nose.

"Jimmy Bird," Jack said, a sardonic note of reproof in his voice. "I had no idea you'd sunk so low."

When Jack bent and scooped up the bundles of cash, the man shrank back from him.

"I see you remember me," Jack said coolly. "We seem destined to meet in circumstances unfavorable to you, don't we? It might be something you want to consider."

"I didn't know she was a friend of yours, Jack. Honest, I didn't."

"Save it, Jimmy." Handing the money to Sydney, Jack crossed his arms over his chest. "Where are the negatives?"

Jimmy Bird's eyes glinted with fear. "Negatives? I ain't got no negatives. I don't know what you're talking about."

"Come on, come on. I haven't got all day. Don't make me convince you that you have them."

With a grimace of pain, the man shook his head and reached into the pocket of his jeans to pull out a cheap white envelope.

"There you go," Jack said, taking them from him. "Now that didn't hurt a bit, did it?"

Sydney stared at Jack, wide-eyed, and when he turned to her, she almost felt afraid of him, herself.

"Come on," he said. "Let's get out of here."

As they stepped through the door, Jack turned back and shot a parting word of warning, "Keep your nose clean, Jimmy."

"Jack," Sydney began as they crossed the parking lot to the Rolls.

"It's all right. You don't have to explain. I think you're crazy. But I realize why you went off on your own like that without telling me." Stopping several paces from the car, he took her in his arms and kissed her. "I know why, Sydney, and I love you for it."

Confused, Sydney stared into his dark eyes, then realized what he was saying. "Jack, don't make me out to be better than I am. Of course I didn't want to involve you. You've done so much for me already. But I have other reasons for not—"

With a finger on her lips, Jack stopped her words. "It's all right." Handing her the two envelopes, he smiled at her tenderly. "You can give them back to your sister if you want, but personally, I think I'd just burn them right here and now."

"My...my sis...my sister," Sydney sputtered.

With a low chuckle, Jack drew her a little closer. "I keep telling you, sweetheart, that I know you better than you think I do. Maybe it takes me a while to figure things out, but eventually, I catch on."

"You've known?"

"For a little while." Taking his lighter out of his jacket pocket, he gave her a charmingly roguish look. "Shall we?"

"Yes," she said, her voice suddenly enthusiastic. "Yes, let's burn them right now."

Holding the envelopes with the tips of his fingers, Jack set the paper on fire, not dropping them until only the fragment of a corner remained.

"Look, Sydney," he said, turning toward the car.

Belinda and Claus hung out the windows, staring at them in stupefaction. Sydney couldn't help laughing at their expressions.

"Who brought the hot dogs?" Jack called.

* * *

It wasn't until they'd begun to pass the outer runways that Sydney realized they were headed, not back to Belinda's, but to the airport. With that realization, a lump formed in the pit of her stomach.

Outside the terminal, she watched as Claus and Jack pulled a multitude of suitcases from the trunk, only half listening to Belinda's light, pleasant chatter. When the suitcases were lined up on the sidewalk, and Belinda had kissed and hugged first Jack, then Sydney, and finally Claus, then driven away, Sydney slowly turned to Jack.

"I think we're going to need more than a few redcaps," Jack was telling Claus. "See about renting a small army."

"Jack?"

"And make sure that two-o'clock flight is still leaving on time."

"Jack?" Sydney repeated.

Turning, he smiled at her. "You don't mind leaving this way, do you? I thought it would be better, just in case Carlton didn't wake up with a sense of humor this morning."

"No. No, I don't mind," Sydney murmured, misery weighing on her like a heavy cloak. "So, I guess . . . I guess this is it."

"Looks that way. Carlton has his two million, plus a lucky dollar bill. Rachel and Tony are poorer, but still alive. And your sister has shed herself of a blackmailer." His smile softened. "Somehow, though, I think we're the ones who've come out the best."

Glancing down at the two steel cases at their feet, she felt the sadness fill her, constricting her throat. "You mean the four million dollars apiece."

He laughed. "No, Sydney. I mean because we have each other."

Sydney's head snapped up, and for the first time she saw that the light in his eyes was not merely desire or admiration. In that second, she saw that it was love.

The sadness in her swelled, threatening to engulf her. Very slowly, she shook her head. "No, Jack. No, we don't."

The smile that graced his lips wavered. "What are you talking about? Of course we do. We'll go back to the island together. We'll be there by tonight and—"

When she continued to shake her head, his smile died completely. He stared at her, suddenly growing still. "What are you saying, Sydney?"

It took every bit of strength she had, but she finally managed to whisper, "I can't. I'm sorry. I can't go with you."

"What do you mean you can't go with me? Of course you can. I've got the tickets. Everything's arranged."

"I'm sorry," she repeated, miserable.

For a long moment, he gazed at her, his dark eyes dazed and uncomprehending. Then he smiled. "Oh, I see. I know what's wrong." Glancing around the busy, noisy airport, he shrugged. "I'd imagined the atmosphere would be a little more romantic when I said this but—well, here goes. I love you, Sydney."

She could feel the tears gathering in the corners of her eyes. To hear those words from him, to hear them now, only made it so much harder. She thought her heart might break.

"Oh, Jack—"

"I think I've loved you from the first moment I saw you. I've never said those words to another woman. I don't say them lightly now. I love you, Sydney, with all my heart. And I want us to be together."

Silently, Sydney gazed into his eyes, her heart heavy with sorrow. Then she looked away.

"I can't. Jack, I can't go with you. Not now. Not yet."

The look that swept across his face was of stunned disbelief. "What? Why not? You feel the same, Sydney. I know you feel the—"

"Jack, please," she cried, raising her hands palm up in a gesture of pleading. "Oh, Jack, don't you see? I've changed. When I first met you, I was frightened and unsure, just as you said I was. But I've changed. I'm not the fat girl inside anymore. I like myself, for the first time in my life. You showed me how, Jack. With you, I've felt beautiful. But I have to know if I can feel that way without you.''

Turning his head, he swallowed hard, and Sydney saw his jaw working as though he was struggling to hold back some frightful emotion.

"Can you understand?" she asked, her voice breaking. "Can you understand that I have to prove that to myself before I can really be sure it's true?"

When he looked at her again, his face had paled and his eyes looked too bright. "No, I don't understand," he said. "I don't understand why you can't come with me. Why can't you be happy with me?"

"Because I need to find out *first* if I can be happy on my own," she cried, desperation in her voice. "Please, Jack. Please try to understand."

Without taking a single step, he seemed to move away from her. "No. No, I can't understand," he said, a thin, hard edge of anger in his voice. "I was an idiot, I see that now. I thought we had more than that, Sydney. I thought what we had meant more to you. As much as it means to me. I thought you felt the same. But I see I was wrong."

Panic fluttered through her, wild and stinging. "Jack, please. That's not what I'm saying. I need time. That's all. I need time to—"

"To what?" His smile was tinged with bitterness. "Time to get over it? Time to convince yourself that you can continue to be alone because it's so much safer than taking a chance on us?"

Sydney gasped. "No, I—"

"Well, *I'm* not afraid, Sydney. I'm not frightened of gambling on you. On us. Take a chance with me, Sydney. Just one more time."

"I can't, Jack. That isn't what this is about. That's not what I'm saying. I just need a little more time."

Reaching out, he gripped her arm with fierce urgency. "Come with me," he implored her. "Come with me now."

"I can't. Jack, I—"

With a quickness that startled her, he released her to bend down and snatch up one of the steel cases and a leather carry-on bag. With bags in hand, he gazed at her with eyes black with pain.

"I'm going, Sydney."

She only stared at him.

"You're going to do this, aren't you? You're going to throw it all away," he said bleakly.

She shook her head silently, her throat too swollen with tears to speak.

"All right then." He straightened his shoulders, his face hard and ashen. "But if you ever change your mind, you know where to find me."

Before she could react, before she could even think, he was stepping away from her. With bowed head, he shouldered his way through the crowd on the sidewalk toward the terminal.

A great wave of grief crashed through her, crushing her. Sydney took an unsteady step forward, raising her hand. "Jack," she called.

But her voice was a barely a whisper, and he was already at the doors of the airport, almost running from her in his haste.

"Jack," she breathed once more, but he was gone.

# 12

On the newly paved veranda at the back of the old governor's mansion, Jack sat in the deck chair and watched the sun set over the Atlantic as he'd done a hundred times before. But the old, soothing peace that used to come to him as night fell evaded him once more. Night was no longer a time when the world became mysterious and new. Night, for him, was haunted now.

Weeks ago, he'd given up trying to sleep in his bed. The longing to feel Sydney beside him on those sheets was too agonizing. Instead, he'd begun to live in the great, cavernous lounge downstairs, still only half-renovated and furnished with just a sofa, and on the veranda where at least the open night sky gave him a little relief from the terrible crushing feeling he carried in his chest all day long.

As the last orange glow of the sun disappeared, Jack sighed and pushed himself out of the chair, went into the house thinking he might get something to eat from Claus in the kitchen, but changed his mind before he'd crossed the room. Carrying a whiskey and soda with him, he went back to the veranda and his deck chair.

And to think that one day, not too long ago, this island and this house had been his salvation, his refuge from the world...his peace. Peace, he thought sardonically. What peace could he ever have with Sydney halfway across the world from him?

Tilting his head, he drank back the whiskey and set the glass on the red-tiled floor. Six weeks ago, his road had seemed so straight and sure, stretching out before him for a million miles. He'd known exactly what he wanted, and where he was going.

And then she'd come along.

He leaned his head back against the chair. He hadn't foreseen that fork in the road. He hadn't known it was waiting for him. But suddenly it was there, all the same. Everything that had been important to him—the building of this resort, the ability to prove to himself that he could make a legitimate success of his life—seemed like nothing next to the loss of Sydney.

If he had known the misery would be this unrelenting, would he have been able to walk away from her that day in Las Vegas?

The lights on the veranda suddenly blazed on, and Jack closed his eyes against the brightness.

"Mr. Ames?" Claus said worriedly.

Jack opened one eye, shaded his face with his hand and looked up. "Yes, Claus? What is it?"

"I made dinner. A nice roast pheasant. You love pheasant."

Jack looked toward the ocean, the new hard-edged sadness in his face made more visible in the veranda lights.

"Thank you, Claus. Maybe later. If you could bring me another whiskey and soda, though..."

"I don't think you need another one."

"Please, Claus. I'm not in the mood to argue with you." Starting to rise, Jack continued, "I'm perfectly capable of getting it myself if you—"

Claus set one huge paw in the center of Jack's chest and pushed him back into his seat. Jack was so astonished he gaped at Claus. He'd always known the man was capable of great physical strength, but to use it against *him?*

"It's not a drink you need," Claus said in his gravelly voice. "Why don't you call her? Go and get her?"

Jack's guts twisted. "You know the answer to that as well as I do," he said wearily. "She'll come when she's ready."

"Sometimes people need persuasion."

For a moment, Jack envisioned himself swooping in, scooping her into his arms and dragging her away, kicking and screaming. Just like any insensitive Neanderthal, Jack thought wryly. He didn't want to admit, even to himself, how close he was to giving it a try.

With his gaze on the horizon, Jack slowly shook his head. "Not yet. When she comes, it has to be because she wants to. I can't force her, Claus. She has to make the decision herself."

"But what if she doesn't?"

The pain seemed to carve a hollow in the very center of him. "She will. She'll come. I'm certain of it."

Sydney shuffled into the dining room in her bathrobe and slippers, her long hair streaming over her shoulders.

"What's for breakfast?" she asked.

Her sister and her brother-in-law exchanged a silent look across the table.

"This is lunch," Sheila said. "You missed breakfast again."

"Really?" Sitting at the table, Sydney peeked under a lid at a platter of succulent, cold roast beef. Her stomach turned.

"Well, I'd better get back to it," Ambrose said self-importantly as he rose. "We're having another big pow-wow at campaign headquarters."

Bending over his wife, he kissed her cheek. Then he startled Sydney by laying a hand on her shoulder before leaving the room.

Picking several celery stalks and a carrot stick from a relish plate, Sydney asked, "So, what's going on today?"

Sheila gave her a long, unreadable look. "We were going to have our hair done. Remember?"

"Oh, yeah. With Morris the Wonder." She bit into the carrot.

"Syd," Sheila began tentatively, as though this was something she'd been rehearsing and had finally gotten up the nerve to say. "What's wrong? Ever since you won that money and quit your job, you've been moping around. Since you came to visit us, you haven't taken out your camera once."

"Are you trying to tell me I'm one of those guests who just won't leave?"

"No. Not at all. I'm thrilled you've come to stay with us. I am. But there's something wrong, Syd. I can see that. What's wrong?"

Surprised, Sydney glanced up. It wasn't like her sister to take much interest in other people's problems.

"Nothing's wrong. Everything's fine." The bitter note in her voice surprised even her. "I mean, I'm beautiful and rich now, aren't I? What could be wrong?"

Sheila glanced down at her plate, toying with her napkin so that her red nails gleamed against the white linen. When she looked up, her mouth was set in that familiar pout Sydney had seen a thousand times before. What was unexpected were her words.

"Why do you do that, Syd? What do you always do that?"

Taken back by her sister's question, Sydney stared. "Do what?"

"Say that everything's fine when everyone knows it's not. You always do that. You always have to be the strong one. The one who has everything together."

Stunned, Sydney held the carrot stick beside her mouth, forgetting to take a bite.

"You never let me in, Syd. I know I'm a scatterbrain a lot of the time, but you're my sister, too. You never tell me anything. You never let me help."

"What are you talking about? I'm letting you pick a new hairstyle for me, aren't I?"

Sheila's bottom lip trembled. "There you go. Doing it again. You're...you're patronizing me. Making everything a joke. All our lives, Syd, just once I wanted you to come to me with a problem. I wanted, just once, to give something back to you. But you won't let me. Because you have to be so...so damned tough."

Sydney gaped. She'd never known her sister to be so upset. "I am not," she said. "I just want to be self-sufficient."

"Why? Why do you have to be?"

"Because." Sydney shrugged uncomfortably. "At least, if I let me down, the only person I have to blame is myself."

It was Sheila's turn to stare. "So you're going to rely only on yourself for the rest of your life. Is that what you're saying?"

"That's the idea of self-sufficiency, I believe," Sydney said flippantly.

With a suddenness that took Sydney completely by surprise, Sheila sprang to her feet, tipping over her chair, and threw her napkin on the table.

"Nobody can be totally self-sufficient, Syd," Sheila exclaimed in distress. "*Nobody*. And in case you didn't know it, it is *not* a weakness to need people."

Storming from the room, she paused at the doorway and turned back. "I love you, Syd, and I need you. And I expect he does, too, whoever he is. But you're too pigheaded to realize that it's okay to need someone yourself. Yes, you might get hurt. We all get hurt sometimes. But you won't even give anyone a chance."

Sydney listened to the sound of her sister's footsteps running through the hall. Glancing down, she saw her hands were trembling.

For nearly an hour, she sat at the table in the dining room, still holding the half-eaten carrot stick. Finally, she rose to her feet to climb the stairs to Sheila's room and, for the first time in her life, poured her heart out to her sister.

\* \* \*

She was wearing the white summer suit with the red braiding, the same outfit she'd worn when he'd first pinned her in front of the mirror and told her to take a good look at herself. Nervously, she smoothed a hand over her hair again, then checked her mascara and lipstick in a small compact.

The taxi she was riding in had no windows. No doors, either. But the yellow fringe that hung from the roof was bright and festive and the taxi driver cheerful and talkative.

Again and again, Sydney swiveled in the seat, staring in amazement at the beauty of the island. Palm trees, graceful and airy, danced in a row down the bumpy dirt road, and everywhere she looked she saw tropical flowers as big as cauliflowers and as colorful as the birds that squawked and soared through the sky.

They'd left behind the small port town with its white-washed buildings and red-clay roofs and climbed into the hills. As they drove, the driver chattered ceaselessly, pointing out one magnificent view after another. Although Sydney nodded and smiled politely, she hardly heard a word he said.

Rounding a bend in the road, Sydney glanced through the undergrowth, and it was then she caught her first glimpse of the old governor's mansion. Sprawling over the hillside, with the glittering blue Atlantic behind it and its walls brilliantly white in the sunshine, the sight took her breath away.

On the edge of her seat, she stared as the taxi wound its way through the tropical jungle.

In the end, she felt they'd reached the resort much too quickly. During the trip, she'd thought they would never arrive. But once the taxi pulled up at the front court, she suddenly feared she wasn't ready.

What would he say to her? Would he be glad she'd come? Or would he be unpleasantly surprised and hastily assume a mask of false welcome that would leave her stunned and crushed?

Climbing from the taxi, she glanced around her as the driver unloaded her suitcases. Once she'd paid the man, she stood uncertainly in the quiet courtyard. Two great, heavy wooden doors, intricately and beautifully carved, stood open in the front of the house.

Leaving her bags on the stone tiles, she went to the doors and peeked in. The room, an enormous, high-ceilinged chamber, was empty and building materials littered the floor. Picking her way around planks and piles of cut stone, she crossed to a wall of French doors.

It was there on the veranda that she found him, leaning against the white stone balustrade and staring pensively out at the sea. He hadn't heard her coming through the house, and she stood awkwardly in the doorway before taking a hesitant step toward him.

Clearing her voice, she called, "I heard there might be a waitressing position open here soon."

He turned then, and for a second she thought he was ill, his face went so white under his tan. He gripped the railing beside him.

Her heart skittered rapidly, weakly in her chest, and she realized she was holding her breath. "I thought," she continued, "that maybe I'd apply."

He was staring at her, his dark eyes black and shadowed. "You've come," he finally said.

With bated breath, she nodded. "Yes, I've come."

In an instant, the strained, ill look was wiped away. The angles of his face, which seemed at first to have grown harsher, softened. In three strides, he was beside her—pulling her against him, burying his face in her hair and crushing her to him.

"You've come," he repeated, clutching her tightly. "Thank God. I knew you would."

"You always seem to know," she said against his chest. "You know me better than I know myself, Jack Ames."

Gripping her arms, he held her away from him, gazing at her, drinking her in as though he couldn't believe he was really seeing her.

"For good?" he asked. "You've come to stay for good?"

"Maybe. Does that mean I get the job?"

"The job?" he asked, his eyes laughing. "But we're not opening for another three months."

The glance she gave him was shy and hopeful. "Maybe there's something else I could do. Another position?"

"Oh, yes. There's been a position open for quite a while. Waiting for you, actually."

"Temporary?"

"Permanent. Permanent and full-time. Think you might be interested?"

Sydney thought her heart might burst with happiness. "I'm interested. I'm very interested."

Drawing her into the circle of his arms, Jack kissed her, long and hard.

"Lady Luck," he murmured against her lips. "I knew from the start you were my Lady Luck."

"Well," she said playfully, "we certainly did win a bundle."

"Oh, no, you don't," he teased back. "You know exactly what I mean. You laid the kiss of Lady Luck on my lips, Sydney, and the word *I* heard wasn't money. It was love."

\* \* \* \* \*

SILHOUETTE®

*Desire*®

CELEBRATION 1000

is on its way
in April, May and June 1996!

Join us for the celebration of Desire's 1000th book!
We'll have

- Book #1000, *Man of Ice* by Diana Palmer in May!

- Best-loved miniseries such as **Hawk's Way**
  by Joan Johnston, and **Daughters of Texas**
  by Annette Broadrick

- Fabulous new writers in our Debut author
  program, where you can collect <u>double</u>
  Pages and Privileges Proofs of Purchase

Plus you can enter our exciting Sweepstakes for
a chance to win a beautiful piece of original
Silhouette Desire cover art or one of many
autographed Silhouette Desire books!

**SILHOUETTE DESIRE'S CELEBRATION 1000**
  ...because the best is yet to come!

## MILLION DOLLAR SWEEPSTAKES
## AND EXTRA BONUS PRIZE DRAWING

SWP-ME96

> "Motherhood is full of love, laughter and sweet surprises. Silhouette's collection is every bit as much fun!"
> —Bestselling author **Ann Major**

This May, treat yourself to...

# WANTED: MOTHER

Silhouette's annual tribute to motherhood takes a new twist in '96 as three sexy single men prepare for fatherhood—and saying "I Do!" This collection makes the perfect gift, not just for moms but for all romance fiction lovers! Written by these captivating authors:

## Annette Broadrick
## Ginna Gray
## Raye Morgan

BOOKS

THE GREATEST GIFT

> "The Mother's Day anthology from Silhouette is the highlight of any romance lover's spring!"
> —Award-winning author **Dallas Schulze**

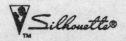

Silhouette®

TM

This April, find out how three unsuspecting couples find themselves caught in the

# The Parent Trap

Sometimes love is a package deal....

Three complete stories by some of your favorite authors—all in one special collection!

**DONOVAN'S PROMISE** by Dallas Schulze
**MILLION DOLLAR BABY** by Lisa Jackson
**HIS CHARIOT AWAITS** by Kasey Michaels

Available this April wherever books are sold.

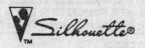

Silhouette®

# As seen on TV!
## *Free Gift Offer*

With a Free Gift proof-of-purchase from any Silhouette® book,
you can receive a beautiful cubic zirconia pendant.

This gorgeous marquise-shaped stone is a genuine cubic
zirconia—accented by an 18" gold tone necklace.

(Approximate retail value $19.95)

## Send for yours today…
### compliments of **Silhouette®**

To receive your free gift, a cubic zirconia pendant, send us one original proof-of-purchase, photocopies not accepted, from the back of any Silhouette Romance™, Silhouette Desire®, Silhouette Special Edition®, Silhouette Intimate Moments® or Silhouette Shadows™ title available in February, March or April at your favorite retail outlet, together with the Free Gift Certificate, plus a check or money order for $1.75 U.S./$2.25 CAN. (do not send cash) to cover postage and handling, payable to Silhouette Free Gift Offer. We will send you the specified gift. Allow 6 to 8 weeks for delivery. Offer good until April 30, 1996 or while quantities last. Offer valid in the U.S. and Canada only.

### *Free Gift Certificate*

Name: _____

Address: _____

City: _____ State/Province: _____ Zip/Postal Code: _____

Mail this certificate, one proof-of-purchase and a check or money order for postage and handling to: SILHOUETTE FREE GIFT OFFER 1996. In the U.S.: 3010 Walden Avenue, P.O. Box 9057, Buffalo NY 14269-9057. In Canada: P.O. Box 622, Fort Erie,

---

**FREE GIFT OFFER**                                         079-KBZ-R

ONE PROOF-OF-PURCHASE

To collect your fabulous FREE GIFT, a cubic zirconia pendant, you must include this original proof-of-purchase for each gift with the properly completed Free Gift Certificate.

---

**079-KBZ-R**

# What do women really want to know?

Trust the world's largest publisher of
women's fiction to tell you.

## HARLEQUIN ULTIMATE GUIDES™

# I CAN FIX THAT

A Guide For Women
Who Want To Do It Themselves

This is the only guide a self-reliant
woman will ever need to deal
with those pesky items that
break, wear out or just don't work
anymore. Chock-full of friendly
advice and straightforward,
step-by-step solutions to the
trials of everyday life in our
gadget-oriented world! So, don't
just sit there wondering how to
fix the VCR—run to your
nearest bookstore for your copy now!

Available this May, at your favorite retail outlet.

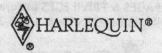

**◆ HARLEQUIN®**

FIX